Venetia fixed her on the professor

"I have given the matter considerable thought," he began, "and it seems to me that it would be to our mutual advantage if you were to become my wife."

Venetia goggled at him. "Your wife?" And then, "You must be joking...."

She saw his eyebrows come together in a heavy frown and went on hastily, "No, all right, you're not joking, only it's so—so unexpected." And when he remained silent, "I don't think I'm the kind of girl you would fall in love with."

"You are laboring under a misapprehension," he observed impatiently. "I have not mentioned falling in love to you, only that you would make me a suitable wife."

Betty Neels is well-known for her romances set in the Netherlands, which is hardly surprising. She married a Dutchman and spent the first twelve years of their marriage living in Holland and working as a nurse. Today she and her husband make their home in a small ancient stone cottage in England's West Country, but they return to Holland often. She loves to explore tiny villages and tour privately owned homes there, in order to lend an air of authenticity to the background of her books.

Books by Betty Neels

HARLEQUIN ROMANCE

2808—TWO WEEKS TO REMEMBER
2824—THE SECRET POOL
2855—STORMY SPRINGTIME
2874—OFF WITH THE OLD LOVE
2891—THE DOUBTFUL MARRIAGE
2914—A GENTLE AWAKENING
2933—THE COURSE OF TRUE LOVE
2956—WHEN TWO PATHS MEET
3004—PARADISE FOR TWO
3024—THE FATEFUL BARGAIN
3036—NO NEED TO SAY GOOD-BYE
3053—THE CHAIN OF DESTINY
3071—HILLTOP TRYST

Don't miss any of our special offers. Write to us at the following address for information on our newest releases.

Harlequin Reader Service
901 Fuhrmann Blvd., P.O. Box 1397, Buffalo, NY 14240
Canadian address: P.O. Box 603,
Fort Erie, Ont. L2A 5X3

THE CONVENIENT WIFE

Betty Neels

Harlequin Books

TORONTO • NEW YORK • LONDON
AMSTERDAM • PARIS • SYDNEY • HAMBURG
STOCKHOLM • ATHENS • TOKYO • MILAN

Original hardcover edition published in 1990
by Mills & Boon Limited

ISBN 0-373-03084-3

Harlequin Romance first edition October 1990

Copyright © 1990 by Betty Neels.
All rights reserved. Except for use in any review, the reproduction or utilization
of this work in whole or in part in any form by any electronic, mechanical or
other means, now known or hereafter invented, including xerography,
photocopying and recording, or in any information storage or retrieval system,
is forbidden without the permission of the publisher, Harlequin Enterprises
Limited, 225 Duncan Mill Road, Don Mills, Ontario, Canada M3B 3K9.

All the characters in this book have no existence outside the imagination of
the author and have no relation whatsoever to anyone bearing the same name
or names. They are not even distantly inspired by any individual known or
unknown to the author, and all incidents are pure invention.

® are Trademarks registered in the United States Patent and Trademark Office
and in other countries.

Printed in U.S.A.

CHAPTER ONE

VENETIA FORBES, sitting at the end of the back row of Casualty's crowded benches, allowed her gaze to roam; it was a nice change from watching the clock on the wall facing her, something she had been doing for over an hour. She was a smallish girl, pleasantly plump, with an ordinary face redeemed from plainness by a pair of magnificent grey eyes, thickly lashed. She had pretty hair of a soft mouse shade which curled on to her shoulders, although at the moment she was so covered in dust and dirt that it was difficult to see that. Her clothes were torn and filthy, and one sleeve had been roughly torn apart so that a first-aid pad could be tied around her forearm, which she held carefully cradled in her other hand. She was a nasty greenish white, but she was apparently composed, unlike her neighbour, a stout woman who was threatening hysterics at any moment and with an eye rapidly turning from an angry red to a rich plum colour. By morning, Venetia thought, it would be an even richer purple.

She glanced at the clock again, and then studied her surroundings. Casualty was bulging at the seams, for not only had those seriously injured in the bomb blast at a nearby Woolworth's been rushed to St Jude's, but the majority of those less seriously hurt as well, St Jude's being the nearest Casualty—a large department, always comfortably occupied, but now crowded to the doors. Most of the people round her had minor wounds—deep scratches and grazes,

5

sprained ankles, perhaps a broken bone or two, and until the really ill victims had been dealt with and warded they would have to possess themselves in patience. There were fifty or sixty people ahead of her, and already a number of them were demanding attention which the hard-pressed nurses and housemen were unable to give.

The woman next to her nudged her bandaged arm, and Venetia went a shade greener and closed her eyes for a moment.

'Sorry, ducks. 'Urt yer arm, 'ave yer? What abart me eye, eh? I've lorst me shoes. 'Ow am I going ter get 'ome, that's what I want ter know?' She surveyed her feet in their remnants of stockings. 'Can't walk like this, can I?'

'I expect they'll send you back in an ambulance.'

'An' when'll that be, I'd like ter know?'

'Not just yet, I'm afraid. They have to attend to the ill people first.'

'Course they do, ducks, but we've been 'ere for getting on for two hours...'

There was a good deal of shuffling from the front bench, and the first of the slightly injured was wheeled away to a cubicle. Venetia, to keep her mind occupied, began doing complicated sums in her head to discover how long it would be before her turn, and looked at the clock once more. Not too long, she hoped. She was feeling sick.

Various persons had been hurrying to and fro past her for ages now, and she had kept her mind occupied by watching them. Quite a few of them she knew, at least by sight—Mr Inglis, the orthopaedic surgeon, his registrar, two consultant surgeons, the senior physician, and any number of house doctors and house surgeons—and she had more than a passing acquaintance with several of the nurses hurrying to and fro, but none of them noticed her. In any case, she reflected, she was probably unrecognisable.

She turned her attention back to the clock and watched the second hand jerking from minute to minute, and she went on staring at it as a very tall man went past and was met by one of the registrars, who ushered him into a cubicle at the far end of the department. She had never spoken to him, only attended his lectures, and she thought it unlikely that she would ever speak to him. Perhaps that was a good thing—from all accounts he was an impatient man, not suffering fools gladly, and with a coldly biting tongue when annoyed. Probably crossed in love, she decided, watching his large back disappear behind the curtains.

It was all of half an hour before she saw him again, and by then the occupants of the benches around her were being dealt with with efficient rapidity. He walked back the way he had come, talking to his registrar, and Venetia's neighbour said, 'Cor—look at 'im. There's an 'andsome bloke.' She put a large hand on Venetia's injured arm; Venetia gave a small, gasping sigh and little beads of sweat shone on her dirty face.

This time, she thought hopelessly, there was nothing for it—she was either going to be sick or faint. She closed her eyes, so she didn't see Professor ter Laan-Luitinga pause by her.

'This girl was here as I came in,' he observed. 'She's all in. I wonder...?' He lifted the pad off her arm and stood studying the splinter of glass which had gone in one side of her forearm and out the other.

Venetia opened her eyes and looked up into his dark face. Very handsome, she thought hazily, and indeed he was, with a high-bridged nose above a rather thin mouth, dark eyes under alarming eyebrows, and a head of dark hair sprinkled with silver. She said clearly, 'I'm so sorry, but I think I'm going to faint.'

And she did. The professor picked her up off the bench. 'An empty cubicle?' he demanded. 'I'll get this thing out—I'll need a local in case she comes round.'

Venetia had never fainted in her life; now she did the thing properly and stayed unconscious for all of three minutes, by which time the professor had made a neat incision, removed the glass shard and given a local injection. Just in time, for she opened her eyes and frowned.

'Lie still,' he told her. 'The glass is out. I'll put in a few stitches as soon as the local acts.' He stared down at her. 'Have you had ATS injections?'

She nodded. 'The last one about three months ago.' She added urgently, 'I'm going to be sick.'

Someone tucked a bowl under her chin and the professor, taking no notice, began his stitching. Presently he cast down his needle. 'That should take care of it,' he observed. 'Go home and go to bed, you'll feel more the thing in the morning. See your own doctor.' He smiled suddenly at her. 'You were in a lot of pain, were you not?' He said to someone she couldn't see, 'Get this young lady back home in an ambulance, will you?' Then he nodded at Venetia, patted her shoulder with a surprisingly gentle hand, and went away, dismissing her from his powerful mind, already battling with the quite different problems of the operation he intended to do on the boy with the damaged brain.

Venetia watched him go, head and huge shoulders above everyone else, his registrar beside him. It must be nice, she reflected, to give orders to people knowing that they would be carried out without any trouble to himself, although, she conceded, it was only fair that anyone with as brilliant a brain as his should be spared the mundane tasks of everyday life.

Her rather hazy thoughts were interrupted by a brisk staff nurse.

'You are to go home and go to bed for the rest of the day. Will you tell me where you live, and I'll see if I can get an ambulance to take you?'

Venetia opened her eyes. 'The nurses' home. Here.'

'For heaven's sake! Why on earth didn't you say so hours ago? Whatever will Sister Bolt say? You should have told someone.'

'Who?' asked Venetia politely. 'When you were all up to your eyes with the badly injured. And I'm perfectly able to go over to the home by myself.'

'Don't you dare. Professor ter Laan-Luitinga will raise the roof in his nasty cold way if he hears that he hasn't been obeyed to the letter. I'll fetch Sister Bolt.'

Venetia closed her eyes again, trying to shut out a threatening headache. Sister Bolt was a veteran of St Jude's and, although Venetia had never worked in Casualty, she knew that its senior sister had a Tartar's reputation. It was therefore surprising when that lady's amazingly sympathetic voice made her open her eyes once more.

'Nurse? What is your name, and which ward are you on?'

'Forbes, Sister and I'm on Watts Ward.'

'You will stay here until the home warden comes for you. I will have a word with her. You fainted.'

'Only because someone accidentally leaned on the splinter, Sister.'

Sister Bolt said kindly, 'You poor child. Very painful. You had better have the rest of the day off.

Eight stitches inserted by Professor ter Laan-
Luitinga...' She uttered the words as though con-
ferring an honour upon Venetia, and went on, 'Did
you become unconscious when the bomb exploded,
Nurse?'

Venetia drew her mousy brows together, thinking
hard. 'No, Sister. It surprised me, and I was blown
off my feet, but there was a stand of winter woollies
by me and they fell on top of me, so, except for the
glass, I'm perfectly all right.' She added apologetically, 'I do have a headache.'

'I'm not surprised. The professor has left instructions as to your medication. When you have been
bathed clean and are in bed you will be given what
he has ordered.'

Sister Bolt sailed away, and very shortly the warden
arrived. She was a nice, cosy, middle-aged lady who
clucked sympathetically over Venetia and hovered
round in a motherly fashion while she was transferred
to a wheelchair, wheeled briskly into a lift, and then
over the bridge which separated the hospital from the
nurses' home. Her arm began to hurt, and she was
grateful to Miss Vale for the speed with which she got
her into a bath, where she was soaped and sponged
and then sat with her eyes obediently shut while her
hair was washed. She felt much better when she was
clean once more, and as Miss Vale turned back her
bed she said, 'I do hope all the other people in Cas
have someone to help them.'

'You may depend upon it,' said Miss Vale cheerfully. 'In you get, and I'm going to get you a nice cup
of tea and some toast and give you those pills. You'll
feel as right as rain when you've had a good sleep.'

So Venetia had her tea, nibbled at the toast and
took her pills, and presently she slept. The October

afternoon was sliding into dusk when she woke to find Sister Giles from her ward standing at the end of her bed.

'Feeling better?'

She was another nice person, thought Venetia, still half asleep. A bit brisk, but perhaps one got like that when one had been running a busy surgical ward for years.

'How's that arm?'

Venetia levered herself up in bed. 'Quite comfy, thank you, Sister.'

'You're on duty at seven-thirty tomorrow. I can't spare you for two days off, but take tomorrow and come on duty the day after, Nurse. The ward's bulging, and I'm having to cut off-duty for a few days.'

'I'm sure I could come on duty tomorrow, Sister——'

'If anything were to go wrong with your arm Professor ter Laan-Luitinga would be most annoyed. The day after will do; there's quite a lot you can do with one arm.' She added with kindly briskness, 'Bad luck, Nurse Forbes. Luckily it's no worse.' She breezed to the door. 'They're bringing you something to eat. Have a quiet day tomorrow.'

The prospect of a day in bed was inviting, the prospect of a meal even more so. When Miss Vale came presently with chicken and creamed potatoes, and a delicious cold pudding which Venetia felt sure she must have pinched from the doctors' supper table, she ate the lot. When the day staff came off duty various of her friends came to see her and, over cups of tea, discussed the day's excitement, sympathised with her and expressed envy that she had been stitched by the professor, who, as one of her friends pointed out, concerned himself with complicated operations on brains and left the easy stuff to lesser men. 'Gosh,' she added, 'it must have been worth it. Did he say anything?'

'He told me to lie still.'

Her friends smiled at her in an indulgent fashion. Venetia was well liked both by her second-year set and by those junior and senior to her. She was good-natured and hard-working, and not in the least interested in catching the eye of any one of the house doctors, and when someone pointed this out to her she merely said that she hadn't time. 'I simply must get trained and get on the register,' she had pointed out. 'Besides, I'm not very exciting to look at, am I?'

A truth which her friends kindly denied while privately agreeing with her.

'I cannot think,' she observed to her companions over a last very strong cup of tea, 'why everyone is so scared of Professor ter Laan-Luitinga. He's only a man, after all, and he doesn't even live here. I mean, he's kind of international, isn't he? Here today and gone tomorrow.'

Caroline Webster, the acknowledged beauty of their set, spoke kindly because she liked Venetia. 'If only he'd stay for a month or two instead of the odd week here and there, Venetia darling. He isn't only a man, he's every girl's dream.' She peered at her pretty face in Venetia's dressing-table looking-glass. 'I wonder if he's married, or has a girl? Such a pity that no one knows a thing about him.'

Someone asked, 'Are you sure that's all he said to you, Venetia?'

'Oh, he asked if I'd had ATS injections.'

'What a waste,' moaned Caroline. 'Couldn't you think of something to say?'

'No, and I was being sick...'

Horrified laughter greeted her, so loud that the night sister, coming to see that Venetia was all right, bade them all go to their rooms and stay there. She offered Venetia a pill, watched her swallow it and went away again, and Venetia went thankfully to sleep once more.

She felt fine in the morning; her arm was sore and stiff, but her headache had gone. She ate the breakfast brought to her and then got up and trailed around in her dressing-gown, sharing elevenses with those of her firm friends who were off duty, watching TV, and doing her nails. Her hands were scratched and grazed, and she was surprised to find that there were bruises on her person, most of them, luckily, out of sight. Her face was scratched as well, and she spent some time rubbing in a cream guaranteed to give instant beauty, offered to her by the generous Caroline. It made very little difference to her ordinary features, and since she had a lovely complexion already it did little good, although it did a lot for her ego.

She went on duty the next morning, and since the ward was still extremely busy there was plenty for her to do, even with one hand: TPRs, adjusting drips, feeding patients, helping the hard-pressed staff nurses with dressings. The day passed very quickly, and although she was late off duty it was still not quite six o'clock when she left the ward.

Her arm was aching now, and she thought thankfully of her bed. She would go to first supper and then get between the sheets. The thought sent her hurrying down the stone staircase and into the main corridor which ran from end to end of the hospital. She was almost at its end when Professor ter Laan-Luitinga turned the corner, walking slowly, a sheaf of papers under one arm, and deep in thought. So deep, she just hoped that he wouldn't see her.

It wasn't until he had passed her that she was brought to a halt by his voice.

'Nurse—wait.'

She turned reluctantly, but stayed where she was.

'Where have I seen you before?' His eyes lighted on the wide strapping on her arm. 'Good lord, who would have thought it?'

A remark which she took in good part; she must have been unrecognisable in Casualty. 'Well, I'm clean now,' she pointed out matter-of-factly, and added a hasty, 'sir'.

His alarming eyebrows drew together. 'Why are you on duty?'

'Well, the ward's awfully busy, and there aren't enough of us to go round.' She smiled at him reassuringly. 'But we can manage. I'm sure you have plenty to worry you, too. I hope that boy is going to do——'

'Yes, eventually.'

'Oh, good. I expect you are very tired,' she added kindly, 'operating and all that. I dare say you could do with a good sleep.'

He stared down at her over his commanding nose. 'When I need advice, Nurse, I will ask you for it.'

His astounded stare at her 'Oh, good,' reminded her to add 'sir' again.

He turned on his heel, and then paused. 'Your name, Nurse?'

'Forbes, Venetia Forbes.' She added, 'I'm not supposed to speak to consultants—I'm only just second year, you see.'

'Pray accept my apologies for making it necessary for you to address me, Nurse Forbes.'

She gave him another smile. 'Well, of course, I will. I think it's very handsome of you to say that. I mean, you don't even need to notice me...'

'I am relieved to hear that.' He gave her a frowning nod and walked away.

She watched his vast person disappearing down the corridor until he turned a corner. 'Very testy,' she declared to the emptiness around her. 'I dare say he'd rather be in Holland—perhaps he's got a wife and children there. Poor fellow.'

The poor fellow, discussing with his registrar the finer points of the craniotomy he was to perform on the following morning, paused suddenly to ask, 'Do you know of a Nurse Forbes, Arthur?'

If Arthur Miles was surprised, he concealed it nicely. 'Venetia Forbes? First or second year nurse on the men's surgical. You stitched her arm in Cas; a glass splinter, if you remember, sir.'

'I remember.'

'Nice little thing, by all accounts. On the plain side, but you must have seen that. Liked by everyone; no wiles, and a bit shy, though she can be remarkably plain-spoken.'

'Indeed?' The professor lost all interest. 'Now, I thought I'd try that new drill...'

Venetia had gone on her way to the nurses' home, to gossip with her friends until it was time for supper, and then retire to her room to drink tea with those of them who weren't going out for the evening. Almost all her friends had some kind of love-affair in progress and, since she made a good listener, she knew the ins and outs of them all, but if she felt that she was missing romance she never said so. To anyone who asked her she replied that she was quite happy to visit her granny on her days off, and in her off-

duty to visit the art galleries and museums easily
reached by bus. They made a nice change from the
dull streets encircling the hospital in the east end of
London; they didn't cost much, either.

She always went to her grandmother's house on her
days off. A small, red brick cottage in a row of similar
ones, tucked away behind the opulent avenues of
Hampstead, it had been home for her for the last five
or six years, ever since her mother and father had
been killed in a car accident. She had no brothers or
sisters, and, for that matter, no uncles or aunts, either.
Save for a cousin of her father's whom she had never
met, and who lived somewhere in Yorkshire, she and
her grandmother were without kith and kin. Her
grandmother hadn't always lived there; when Venetia
was very small she had gone with her mother and
father to visit her grandparents at a nice old house on
the edge of a Sussex village, but when her grandfather
had died a good deal of his income had died with
him, and her grandmother had moved to the little
house she now lived in to be near Venetia's parents,
who lived in a pleasant house on the other side of the
Heath. It wasn't until after their deaths that she discovered that the house had been rented, and what
money there was was barely enough to feed and clothe
her. All the same, her grandmother had insisted that
she should continue at school until she had her A
levels. She was eighteen by then, and, although she
had been offered a place at one of the lesser univer-
sities, she had got a paid job instead as a receptionist
to a team of doctors and then, almost two years ago,
she had persuaded her grandmother to let her train
as a nurse.

She had had no regrets; she enjoyed her work and,
being a friendly soul, had no trouble in making

friends. The patients liked her, too, for she was patient and good-tempered and most sympathetic without being sentimental. The pay wasn't very much, for she had to pay board and lodging to the hospital, but there was enough over to buy clothes and help out her grandmother's small income. And it would get better—in a little over a year she would be trained, with more freedom, more money and a chance to work where she fancied.

It was three days later that she met the professor again. She had raced off duty at five o'clock, changed into a sweater and skirt, brushed her hair and tied it back, packed what she would need for a couple of days into a big shoulder-bag, dragged on her jacket and sped down to the entrance. The rush hour was on and she would have to get into a queue for a bus, but she would still be home in time for supper.

She was half-way across the vast expanse of the entrance hall when she saw the professor making for the door from the other side—the side sacred to consultants, the hospital secretary's office and the boardroom. He was going fast, and if she slowed her steps there would be no need to encounter him—on the other hand, if she just hurried more she might slip through the door ahead of him. The quicker she got to the bus stop the better the chance of getting on a bus at this hour of day.

As it turned out they arrived at the door together, and to her annoyance he opened it for her and then stood so that she couldn't get past him.

'Ah, Nurse Forbes. You have had the stitches out?'

'Thank you, yes, sir. You stitched it beautifully; there'll be almost no scar.'

His firm mouth twitched. 'I do my best. Why are you dancing around like that? Are you in a hurry?'

She had indeed been edging round him. 'I'm going to catch a bus.'

'Where to?'

It was none of his business, but she said politely, 'Hampstead.'

'Ah—Hampstead. I'm just about to drive myself there; may I offer you a lift?'

'Well,' said Venetia, 'it's very kind of you, sir, but I'm not sure...'

He hadn't listened to a word. She was swept outside into the courtyard, and walked across to where a dark blue Bentley was parked. 'Get in,' he said, and, since it was obvious to her that he meant exactly what he said, she got in.

'Where do you live?'

He had inched the car into the rush-hour traffic and had turned the nose to the west.

'If you would drop me off in any part of Hampstead...' began Venetia.

'Don't be ridiculous. Where do you live?'

'Do you talk to everyone in such a manner?' asked Venetia, quite forgetting who he was. 'Or perhaps,' she went on thoughtfully, 'you're tired after a long day's work.'

'Think whatever you wish, Nurse. Where do you live?'

'Percy Lane. It's behind——'

'I know where it is. Are you married or—er—having a lasting relationship with some young man?'

They were driving through Holborn, and then on towards Primrose Hill; they would be in Hampstead very soon now. 'No,' she said quietly, 'I'm not married, and I haven't a boyfriend or anything like that. I live with my granny, at least for my days off and my holidays.'

'No parents or brothers or sisters?'

'No.'

He had nothing more to say, and she sat quietly, enjoying the comfort of the big, smooth car until he slowed and turned into Percy Lane. 'Which house?'

'Number fourteen, on the left half-way down.'

He slid to a halt, leaned across her and opened the door and undid her seat-belt, then got out himself and hauled her bag from the back of the car. 'Enjoy your days off.' He sounded as though he didn't much care whether she did or not. 'Goodnight, Nurse.'

'Goodnight, and thank you, sir.' She looked up into his face and smiled a little. He looked tired; perhaps that was why he looked austere and impatient whenever she had encountered him. She said kindly, 'You must be glad to be going home; you look tired, sir.'

His mouth twisted into a sneer. 'I am touched by your solicitude, Nurse. Quite wasted upon me, I'm afraid.'

He got back into the car and drove away, and she watched the car until it had turned back into the wide avenue at the end of the lane, and then beat a tattoo on the door of the little house behind her.

It was opened immediately. 'Come in, child. How nice to see you. Who was that? A Bentley, too!'

Venetia kissed her grandmother, a small, elderly lady with the same nondescript features as her granddaughter, and with the same beautiful eyes. 'Nice to be home, Granny. That was Professor ter Laan-Luitinga. He's an honorary brain surgeon who comes to operate here from time to time. He met me at the door and offered me a lift.'

Her grandmother ushered her into the little sitting-room. 'Nice of him, darling. Supper won't be long.

Leave everything in the hall, you can go to your room later.'

She cast a quick look at her granddaughter's face. She was way behind with modern ways and habits, but in her elderly view it seemed strange that a member of the consultant staff should offer a lift to a student nurse he would probably know nothing of. Unless, of course, they had met already.

She took her usual high-backed chair in the pleasant room, remembering that she hadn't heard from Venetia for some days, and there had been that bomb...

'Did you see anything of that bomb outrage?' she asked. 'There must have been any number of casualties, and it was close to St Jude's.'

'Well, actually, I was in Woolworth's when it went off, Granny. I was one of the lucky ones, though— just cut my arm a little. Professor ter Laan-Luitinga stitched it for me, and it's perfectly all right.'

Her grandmother gave a small sigh of satisfaction. So that was why...

'Let me see it, Venetia.'

The scar was examined, and pronounced a very neat piece of needlework. 'Couldn't have done it better myself,' said her grandmother. 'I thought you said he was a brain surgeon.'

'Well, yes, he is. He just happened to go past while I was waiting in Casualty.'

'How very fortunate, child.' Her grandmother, a great knitter, began to turn the heel of a sock she was making. 'Now tell me what you've been doing since I saw you last.'

Venetia's two days off passed quickly. There was nothing exciting to do, but she didn't mind—it was nice just to potter round the little house, go shopping with her grandmother, and sit round the fire in the evening listening to her reminiscing about Venetia's mother and father. She had been very happy in those days, and remembering them made her sad, but, as her grandmother had said, life had to go on, and the sooner she was trained with the certainty of a secure job, the better. 'I shan't live forever,' said her grandmother, 'and there won't be much for you, child. I've borrowed on this house, so there will be only a fraction of its worth to come to you. It's not what I would have wished.'

Venetia had assured her that she had no need to worry; she already paid some of her salary towards household expenses, and in another year or two she would earn sufficient to look after the pair of them.

St Jude's loomed inhospitably out of the evening mist when she went back the following day. The bus had been packed, and when she got out of it the sight of the narrow, shabby streets around her sent her usually cheerful heart plummeting down into her sensible shoes. Perhaps when she had trained she would be able to find a job away from London, somewhere from where she could still get to Hampstead to visit Granny, but where there were trees and fields and one could hear the birds singing.

The alternative, of course, was to find a millionaire and marry him. She laughed at the very idea, and Sedgwick, the head porter, looked up from his scrutiny of the evening paper.

'Feeling 'appy, Nurse? On men's surgical, aren't you? 'Ad three nasty cases in today—motorbikes— and there's another just in, not 'alf an hour ago.'

Venetia poked her head through his little window. 'What a welcome!' she observed cheerfully. 'For two pins I'd turn round and go home again.'

She went unhurriedly across the entrance hall and down the passage to the nurses' home, where she spent a pleasant hour before bed drinking tea and catching up on the hospital gossip with various of her friends.

There was precious little time to gossip on the following day; the ward was full and, just as Sedgwick had said, the three cases which had been admitted were nasty ones, for not only were they badly injured, they were uncouth youths who raved and shouted and used language which Venetia, for one, didn't always understand—which was perhaps a good thing. And the fourth case was developing symptoms of a hidden head injury as well as internal injuries. Sister Giles sent for Arthur Miles, who spent a long time examining the man and then disappeared into her office to telephone, and fifteen minutes later Professor ter Laan-Luitinga arrived.

Venetia, trotting briskly out of a dressing-room with a tray of dressings, managed to halt within a few inches of him, and even then she trod on the toe of his large, beautifully polished shoe.

'Oops, so sorry, sir!' She smiled widely at him, quite forgetting that when they had last met he had snubbed her quite nastily. He snubbed her now, not by saying anything—his nod was glacial, his dark eyes cold, dismissing her with a glance.

She went on her way, reflecting reasonably that there was no earthly reason why he should so much as smile at her. All the same, he had no need to look as though she weren't there. She handed over the dressings to Staff Nurse Thomas, who was tall and thin, wore a perpetually cross expression and, although very competent, intimidated the patients. The elderly man having his dressing changed grinned at Venetia as she stood by the trolley ready to pass anything needed; a nice little thing, he reflected, never too busy to turn a pillow or fetch more water. He was on the point of exchanging a joke with her when Sister Giles poked her head round the curtains. 'Nurse Forbes, Professor ter Laan-Luitinga wants that patient transferred to his unit now. He intends to operate this afternoon. Pack up everything, will you, and go with the patient and hand him over.'

There wasn't much to pack up, and since the patient was becoming more and more drowsy there was no use in checking his few possessions with him. Venetia made a tidy packet, helped the porters get him on to the trolley, accompanied them to the lift and was whisked to the fifth floor which was the professor's domain when he was at the hospital. He came out of IC as they proceeded down the wide corridor to the end cubicle and stood watching them. Venetia took care not to look at him and, once the patient was in his bed, busied herself arranging this and that in his locker. Then she stood waiting until a nurse came to relieve her.

The professor came instead. 'You will be good enough to stay with this patient, Nurse. You will be relieved shortly. Ring the panic bell if you find it necessary. Sister will be here presently.'

'Sister Giles is expecting me back, sir.'

'She shall be informed.'

He went away and she glanced uneasily at the patient. It was a relief when the junior sister came in, made sure that he was lying correctly, checked that Venetia knew what to do if he showed signs of distress, and assured her that someone would come the moment she pressed the bell. 'We're rushed off our feet,' she explained. 'Just as soon as there's a nurse free, she'll take over.'

But the professor came first, and one of the an-
aesthetists was with him. He paused when he saw
Venetia, his dark face frowning. 'You're still here,
Nurse?'

'Well, there is no one else, sir,' she pointed out
matter-of-factly, and listened to his irritable rum-
blings. He must be worn to the bone, she reflected.
A professor of surgery he might be, but he was also
at everyone's beck and call. She hoped that he had a
nice home life to make up for it . . .

He pressed the panic bell; there was a flurry of feet
along the corridor, and Sister and a nurse came in
smartly.

'There is no panic, Sister, but be good enough to
find an experienced nurse to remain with this patient.'
His voice was chillingly polite, and Sister shot a look
at Venetia as though she were to blame. 'I thought,'
went on the professor smoothly, 'that I had made it
clear that he needs a trained eye.' His own eye lighted
on Venetia. 'Go back to your ward, if you please,
Nurse.'

She was only too glad to do so. Worn to the bone
he might be, she muttered savagely, racing down
several flights of stairs, but civil he was not. Downright rude, in fact. It was with regret that she conceded
that she wasn't in a position to tell him so.

CHAPTER TWO

OCTOBER ebbed slowly into November, bringing with it chilly rain and wind and darkening mornings. Watts Ward was busy and Venetia trotted to and fro, and when her days off came round went thankfully to the cottage in Percy Lane. It was pleasant to get up in her own room in the morning and make tea for her grandmother and do the shopping, and all without having to keep an anxious eye on the clock. In the evenings they sat by the fire and talked, which was pleasant, and her grandmother knitted and Venetia wound wool or did nothing at all.

She had seen nothing of the professor. He came very seldom to Watts Ward, but he was to be glimpsed from time to time going in or out of the hospital. It was Caroline who told her that he had gone back to Holland. 'What a lovely life,' she added. 'Think of all the people he meets. He must be rolling in cash— I bet he's got a marvellous house somewhere.'

'It's to be hoped that he has,' said Venetia sedately. 'If he's married his wife and children will need a roof over their heads.'

Caroline giggled. 'Venetia darling, there's not a scrap of romance in you. I've got a date with one of the housemen in his team—I'm going to find out something more about our professor.'

Venetia raised her eyebrows and then smiled. 'I dare say if I were as pretty as you, Caro, I'd do that, too.'

But Caroline discovered nothing of the professor's private life. Tim Dobson either didn't know or wasn't going to tell, and Venetia, caught up in a week even busier than usual, forgot to ask.

She felt that days off made a more than welcome break, even when it meant queueing in the cold rain for a bus after a long day. Venetia, struggling off the bus, made for Percy Lane as fast as her tired feet would allow, thinking of her supper and her grandmother's welcome. It surprised her to see that the cottage was in darkness, and when no one answered the door she had a moment's apprehension, which she explained away with her usual common sense. Her grandmother had a number of friends living in Hampstead, and it was barely seven o'clock—she could have lingered after having tea with one of them. She got out her key, opened the door and let herself into the narrow hall.

As she switched on the light she called, 'Granny,' but the little house was silent. She put down her bag and went into the sitting-room, turning on the light as she did so. The fire had burned low and her grandmother was sitting in her chair, her knitting in her lap, and Venetia knew before she reached her and felt for her pulse that she wouldn't be able to find it. She said, 'Granny?' again in a frightened voice, and put her young arms around the elderly shoulders. She stayed like that for a few minutes, thrusting back grief. That could come later...

There was no telephone in the cottage. She crossed the road to one of the neighbours and phoned her grandmother's doctor, and then went back and waited quietly for him to come, sitting very still, her granny's hand in hers.

It was the end of the month before the professor returned to St Jude's, and, after discussing the operation he intended doing on the following day, he got into his car and drove himself to his house. He was going through Hampstead when he saw Percy Lane's narrow opening, and on an impulse he turned the car into it. He wasn't sure why he was going—Venetia probably wouldn't be there. He was being foolish, and he was annoyed at that.

There was a light shining between the drawn curtains and the front door was open. He got out of the car and pushed the door wider, and noticed then that there was a house agent's board fastened on to the wall beside it. He said, 'Venetia, I'm coming in,' and pushed the sitting-room door open. She was sitting at the little round table by the window, her hands in her lap, and the face she turned to him was so white and weary that he said quickly, 'What's the matter? Are you ill?' His dark eyes swept round the little room; it was scrupulously tidy, and also very cold. 'Your grandmother?' he asked.

Venetia supposed that she should have felt surprise at seeing him, but she didn't. She said in her quiet way, 'She died rather suddenly, two weeks ago.'

'My poor girl.' He undid his coat, tossed his gloves on to the table and sat down opposite her. 'The house is up for sale. Why are you sitting here in the cold alone?'

She said steadily, 'Well, you see, this house doesn't belong to Granny now—there was some arrangement she made a long time ago—she sold it to some kind of company, and they let her have the money for it then so that she had an income.' She added seriously, 'The rates are rather high, you know, and there wasn't any other money, only her pension. That's why I'm here—someone's coming with some papers for me to sign . . .'

'Have you no solicitor?'

'Oh, yes, but you see it wasn't convenient for him to come here in the evening, and he said it was all right for me to sign them.' She went on in her sensible way, 'The furniture is mine.'

'You have family?'

'No. At least, only a cousin of my father, whom I've never met. He and my father didn't like each other, and I don't suppose he would want to hear from me.'

He got up and shut the door. 'When is this man coming?'

She glanced at the clock on the mantelpiece. 'Now, if he's punctual. Can I get you a cup of tea? I'm so sorry I didn't ask you . . .'

Someone knocked on the door and he got up. 'I'll answer that. Are you having days off?' And when she nodded he added, 'And sleeping here?'

'They said I could stay until the end of the month. There are things to pack up.'

He nodded and went to the front door, and presently he ushered in a businesslike-looking man with a briefcase. 'Go ahead,' he invited him. 'I'm merely here in an advisory capacity.'

A remark which made Venetia blink with surprise. She still wasn't thinking straight, but she was conscious of relief that the professor should have appeared on her doorstep just when she knew she needed someone. She wished the man good evening, and set herself to read the papers he offered her. Then she passed them over to the professor, who read them, too. They were quite in order, and it was no good pointing out that if the house had been Venetia's on her grandmother's death she would have been able to sell it for three times the amount her grandmother had received for it.

Venetia sighed, offered tea and was refused, and watched the professor see the man to the door. When he came back into the room she got up.

'Thank you very much, Professor,' she said politely. 'It was very kind of you to stay. Now I have only to pack up and get somewhere to store the furniture.' She added, unconsciously wistful, 'Would you like a cup of tea before you go?'

'No. Get whatever you need for the night. You're coming back with me.'

Her white face flushed faintly. 'Indeed, I am not, Professor. It is very kind of you to suggest it——'

'I'm not being kind, I'm being sensible. You can't stay alone. My housekeeper will look after you, and you can return in the morning and do whatever you have to do.'

He sounded reassuringly disinterested.

'But won't it interfere with your evening?'

'Why should it? I'm going out to dinner, and shall not be back until late, and I'm operating in the morning. I suggest that you spend your two nights at my house and come and go as you please.' He turned a frowning look upon her. 'I'm already a little late.'

Put like that, there wasn't much that she could do about it and, indeed, she hadn't quite regained her usual independent spirit. She pushed a few things into her overnight bag, locked up and put on her coat, to be bustled out and into the Bentley, greatly to the interest of the neighbours.

It was a dark, misty evening and later there would be a frost. Venetia was grateful for the warmth of the big car, and at the same time realised that she was hungry. She hadn't waited for tea at the hospital, and her midday dinner had been gobbled because she had been delayed on the ward by old Mr Thirsk, who was recovering from a stomach operation and had mislaid his glasses. It had taken her a few minutes to find them among the bedclothes, and by then his neighbour was demanding that his water jug be filled. Somehow her hunger was the last straw; she had just parted with what had been her home for some years, and she had very little idea what to do next. Go on nursing, of course, but there was the question of the furniture, and the solicitor had mentioned several outstanding bills. To her horrified shame her eyes filled with tears. They dripped down her cheeks, getting worse every moment. She put out her tongue and did her best to catch them, and sniffed discreetly, but she was quite unable to stop. It was a good thing that her companion was looking ahead of him. She turned her head away and gazed unseeingly out of the window.

The professor had turned into a wide road skirting the Heath, with houses standing well back, surrounded by large gardens, overlooking the fields and trees. He turned into an open gateway and stopped before the lighted porch of the house at the very end of the road, switched off the engine and asked quietly, 'Why are you crying, Venetia?' At the same time he offered her a handkerchief.

She mopped her eyes, blew her small nose defiantly, and said in a sodden voice, 'You're so kind.' She looked at him over the hanky. 'I'm very sorry— Mother always said that nothing annoyed a man more than women weeping.' She gave a gulp and scrubbed at her face. 'It's just that it's one thing on top of another,' she mumbled.

He put out an arm and drew her close so that her head was on his shoulder. He didn't say anything, but the comfort of it started her weeping once more. He let her cry for several minutes and then said, 'We'll sort things out tomorrow. I'll be home after lunch for a couple of hours. I think it will be best if you stay here until I get back, then we can talk about it. It will be easier with two.'

She sniffed into his coat. 'I'm not usually so silly, but it was all a bit sudden.'

'And you had no one to turn to,' he said softly. He disentangled her from his shoulder and undid her seat-belt, then got out to open her door. 'Mrs Todd will look after you and give you supper.' He had opened the door with his key, and ushered her inside. The hall was large and square, lit by a crystal chandelier hanging from a plastered ceiling, and a curved staircase rose from one side. There were a number of doors leading from it, and from one of these came a small, round woman with grey hair piled high in elaborate rolls, wearing a neat dark dress.

'There you are, sir.' She trotted to meet them. 'Todd's laid out your things. And can I get you anything...?' Her small twinkling eyes studied Venetia.

'Mrs Todd, I've brought Miss Venetia Forbes back here for a couple of nights. Will you see that she has supper? And give her the room overlooking the back garden, will you? Perhaps you would take her there now, and then come back to me.'

Mrs Todd smiled and nodded. 'Right, sir. If Miss Forbes would like to come upstairs...'

It was a lovely house, thought Venetia, following Mrs Todd obediently. Not only lovely to look at, but it felt...she sought for a word...like home, warm and welcoming and softly lit. She had no doubt,

either, that it was run on oiled wheels. She sighed and
Mrs Todd turned round to say kindly, 'You're tired,
miss. I can see that. A nice supper and then bed—
there's nothing like a night's sleep to get you on your
feet again.'

She opened a door on the balcony above the
staircase and ushered Venetia inside. The room was
quite large, with a large window draped in old rose
chintz; the counterpane on the bed matched exactly,
and the rose colour was repeated on the small armchair and the bedside lights. The carpet was thick, a
rich cream colour which, reflected Venetia, her
housewifely instincts aroused, would be quite a
problem to keep pristine. She glanced guiltily at her
own shoes and then apologetically at Mrs Todd, who
only smiled in a cosy way and led her into the ad-
joining bathroom.

'You just tidy yourself, miss, and then come downstairs. Todd'll be there to show you where to go. And
just you ask me if there's anything you need.'

Examining the dressing-table, a dainty affair of
maple wood, and then the bathroom, Venetia decided
that someone had provided everything a girl could
want cosmetic-wise. It would be lovely to use them,
but she decided against that; she was only there for
a couple of nights, and she supposed that anything
used, however sparingly, would have to be replaced.
She washed her face and hands, powdered her prosaic
features, tidied her hair and went down the stairs.

Todd was waiting for her, a small round man,
exactly right for Mrs Todd, but with a great deal of
dignity. He bade her good evening, opened a door
and silently ushered her into what she supposed was
the drawing-room. It extended from the front of the
house to the back, its parquet floor strewn with silky

rugs, and a number of comfortable armchairs and sofas disposed about it. The professor rose from an outsize chair by the open fire and came to meet her. 'Ah—just time for us to have a drink before I go out. I made it clear that you are to spend your nights off duty here? You will have a good deal to do during the next few days. It would be satisfactory if you could settle everything before you go back to St Jude's.'

He handed her a glass of sherry and sat down opposite her chair. 'I shall be here shortly after two o'clock tomorrow. It would be helpful if you had decided by then exactly what you intend to do with your possessions, so that arrangements can be made.'

She took a sip of sherry and said thoughtfully, 'You are awfully kind, Professor, but please don't bother. I'm very grateful for your hospitality, but I'll manage quite well——'

'Are you telling me not to interfere?' His voice was chilly.

'My goodness me, no. Only I think I've been enough bother to you already.'

'Which is no reason for us to leave things half done.'

A remark which struck her as decidedly indifferent to her feelings, to say the least.

He went away presently with a polite wish that she should enjoy her evening and go to bed at a reasonably early hour, and she in her turn was invited by Todd to accompany him to a pleasant room at the back of the house, where she dined deliciously and in solitary state, and then, not wishing to disrupt the household more than necessary, elected to go to bed.

To her surprise the professor was in the hall, magnificent in a dinner-jacket and looking ill-tempered. He was listening to someone on the telephone, and said curtly, 'I have been delayed, unavoidably so.' He glanced at his watch. 'I should with luck be with you in twenty minutes.' He put down the phone, frowned at her, rumbled something which might have been goodnight, and let himself out of the house.

Venetia stood on the bottom stair and listened to the car being driven away. A staid tabby cat had arranged itself comfortably on one of the high-backed chairs in the hall, and she addressed it for lack of any other audience. 'Poor man. I am being a nuisance, but he didn't have to make it quite so obvious, did he? I dare say that was his girlfriend telling him off.'

The cat settled herself just so and began on a meticulous toilet, and Venetia turned and went upstairs. 'I am lapped in luxury,' she told herself as she went, 'so I have no reason to feel lonely.' But she was.

She spent all of ten minutes wondering about the professor, guessing wildly at his life, wondering, too, whereabouts he lived in Holland. No wife, she decided. Somehow he didn't strike her as the kind of man to leave his wife at home while he took up residence somewhere else for weeks on end. She was inventing a beautiful blonde sitting opposite him in some exclusive restaurant at the very moment when she fell asleep.

A cheerful girl brought her early-morning tea, wished her a good morning and begged her to stay in bed, since Mrs Todd was even then cooking her breakfast and would bring it up herself.

Which that good lady did, not ten minutes later: scrambled eggs, crisp toast, orange juice and a pot of coffee. 'And mind you eat every crumb, miss,' she urged. 'You could do with a bit more flesh on your bones. A nasty time you've been having, by all accounts, and a good lie-in will do you the world of good. There'll be coffee if you want it when you come downstairs, and I'll dish up a nice little lunch at half-past twelve sharp, since the professor expects to be home earlier than he thought. Phoned he did, ten minutes ago. He'll have a sandwich and a glass of beer at the hospital and then come right home.'

Venetia longed to ask questions, there was so much she wanted to know about the professor, but she held her tongue. Mrs Todd was a kind little chatterbox, but she suspected that to chatter about her employer would be the last thing the housekeeper would do.

She ate her breakfast, had a bath—much too hot and lengthy—dressed and went downstairs. Todd, with the cat trailing him, came to meet her in the hall. 'Good morning, miss. The professor asked me to suggest to you that you should decide which firm you wish to employ to dispose of your furniture. It will save time this afternoon, and allow arrangements to be made.'

He opened the door to the room where she had had dinner. There was a fire burning brightly, and coffee on a tray placed invitingly on a drum table, by a small armchair. 'I have put the local telephone directory on the table in the window, miss. Also today's newspaper.'

After the bleak weeks she had struggled through it seemed like a dream world. She sipped coffee and studied the lists of firms who might be suitable. There were one or two things she would like to keep: a papier-mâché work-table which had belonged to her mother, a small collection of her grandmother's books, one or two pieces of silver left from more af-fluent days... She made a tidy list of these, picked out the more modest firms who might dispose of the furniture, and opened the *Daily Telegraph*, suppressing a feeling of guilt because she wasn't going to do anything useful.

She lunched deliciously: watercress soup, cream sitting on its smooth green; a cheese soufflé; baked apple dumplings with a rich custard; and more coffee afterwards. She was just finishing her second cup when the professor walked in. He was followed by Todd, bringing fresh coffee, and sat down at the table. Venetia wished him good afternoon and received a beetle-browed stare. Evidently he was in no need of the niceties of speech; she finished her coffee and waited silently.

'If you have decided what you wish to do with your furniture and who is to deal with it, there is no reason why the business shouldn't be settled at once. Presumably you don't have any more days off for another week?'

'No, I don't. And I should like to get everything settled today and tomorrow. I have chosen a firm I think will do. A local business—perhaps they could collect the furniture before I go back to the hospital.'

He put down his cup. 'Then let us go without delay.'

'Give me two minutes,' begged Venetia, and belted upstairs to fetch her coat and handbag. He was obviously impatient to get the whole business settled; indeed, she suspected that he probably regretted even offering to help her in the first place. Well, two could be businesslike; she nipped down to the hall, intent on getting through the afternoon's business as quickly as possible.

Things went smoothly. At the professor's instigation, someone from the house furnishers she had elected to go to accompanied them to her grandmother's house and, since it was a small place and there wasn't a great deal of furniture, within the hour he had assessed its contents and named a price, with the undertaking that it would be removed on the following day and a cheque for the amount paid to her if she cared to call in the afternoon. Moreover, he offered to store the one or two pieces she wished to keep. The matter nicely settled, they all drove back to his place of business where Venetia arranged to call on the following day.

The professor had had little to say, but what he had said had been very much to the point and with no words wasted. She got back into the car and they drove back to his house and went indoors. In the hall he said, 'I suggest that you telephone your solicitor and anyone else concerned with your affairs. There's a phone in the small sitting-room.' He turned away. 'You will excuse me if I leave you? I have some letters to dictate before I go back to St Jude's.'

'Thank you very much for your help, Professor. I'm very grateful.'

He paused at his study door. 'You have no relations other than your father's cousin who has no interest in you?'

'No.' He was frowning so heavily that she added kindly, 'But it doesn't matter at all, I've lots of friends.'

He nodded. 'I shall be out this evening. Feel free to come and go as you please. You return to your duties tomorrow?'

She made haste to assure him that she would return to the hospital when she had been to receive the cheque from the furniture company. 'I—I've promised to go out in the evening,' she fibbed, in case he might think that she would want to stay for dinner.

He regarded her thoughtfully, aware of her small lie, even guessing why she had told it. 'Just as you wish.' He smiled faintly. 'I dare say that we shall see each other occasionally in St Jude's.'

'Oh, yes, but not to talk to, of course. I'm not supposed to talk to consultants, only to answer them if they ask me something.'

She gave a brisk nod and went upstairs to take off her coat. When she went down again the house was quiet as she went to the small sitting-room and did her telephoning. That done, she sat quietly until Todd came in with the tea-tray and the news that the professor had returned to the hospital and would only come back for a brief visit in order to change for the evening.

She was saved from loneliness by the presence of the cat, who curled up on the chair on the other side of the hearth and went to sleep while she sat with paper and pen, making plans. The money from the furniture sale wasn't a great deal, but she felt emboldened to spend a little of it; she needed new boots for the winter as well as a topcoat. The remainder she would put in the bank to swell her tiny capital against a rainy day.

And tomorrow, she reflected, she would leave during the morning, for she felt that she had tried the professor's hospitable instincts to their limit. She could look at the shops, have a snack lunch, collect her cheque and go back to St Jude's. Having decided things to her satisfaction, she drank the sherry Todd handed to her and sat down to her dinner. It was a pity that her grandmother wasn't there to share the delicious food. For a moment her firmly suppressed grief threatened to engulf her, but Granny had had no time for self-pity. She was young, and once she had trained she would have a safe, interesting job for as long as she wanted, or until she retired, she supposed. She dreamed of marrying, as any girl of her age would, but she had no looks to speak of and, according to her friends at the hospital, looks were of paramount importance when it came to getting a husband.

She was a sensible girl, and she didn't dwell on the lack of romance in her future, but made civil conversation with Todd, who was presiding over her dinner. He excused himself when he had served her pudding, and she heard him talking in the hall, and then the professor's deep voice. Todd came back presently, and after a little while she heard the professor's step in the hall and the sound of the heavy front door being shut.

She explained to Todd when she went down to breakfast that she would be leaving that morning, refusing his offer of a nice lunch, although she agreed that she wouldn't go until he had brought her coffee later on in the morning. And, when it came to the point of leaving, she felt real regret as she thanked the Todds for their kindness; the professor's home had spelt security and calm just when she had needed it. She refused the taxi Todd offered her, and walked to the High Street, where she idled away an hour before having lunch in a small café and then going to collect her cheque. That done, there was nothing to keep her there any longer. She made her way to Percy Lane and found the little house already empty, and, mindful of the solicitor's instructions, left the keys on the sitting-room mantelshelf and then went quickly away, closing the door behind her and not looking back.

In a way it was a relief to be back at work, even though Staff Nurse Thomas was sharper tongued than usual and there were several testy patients who wanted attention all the time, never mind how busy the nurses were.

Of the professor there was no sign. It wasn't for a day or two after her return that Caroline, sharing a pot of tea with her before bed, observed that he had gone back to Holland.

'How do you know?' asked Venetia. 'I mean, you knew last time, too...'

'Tim told me. But he'll be back. I heard Theatre Sister telling Sister Bolt that there was a brain tumour being sent over from Jersey—he's bound to be back to deal with it. It's a teaser, she said, and they always have him over for the nasty ones.'

Two days later she met him in one of the long downstairs corridors. She was on her way to collect a drug which had to be given immediately, and was racing along much too fast. His long arm, shooting out to try to stop her, brought her to a halt.

He had his registrar with him, which probably accounted for his bland, 'Ah, Nurse Forbes. Your domestic difficulties are at an end, I trust?'

'Yes, thank you, sir.' She had gone a little pink with the unexpectedness of the meeting, and when he nodded in a dismissive manner she smiled a little uncertainly at him and hurried off on her errand. Seeing him brought back the memories she had been trying so hard to stifle. All at once she longed for her grandmother and the little house in Hampstead—more than that, she longed for an anchor, somewhere to call home, somewhere to go when she was free. She hadn't moped, she had done her best, spending her free days visiting museums and art galleries, eating economical meals in busy cafés so that she had people around her, assuring her friends when they asked her that she simply loved exploring London, anxious not to infringe upon their kind concern for her. And now the professor was back to upset her. She had some holiday due, she would use some of her little capital and go away. Right away, although just for the moment she had no idea where.

The answer came from an unexpected source the very next day. The professor's registrar stopped her as she was crossing the entrance hall, intent on giving a message to whoever was in the porter's lodge.

'Spare a minute?' he asked pleasantly, and, since he had always been friendly and she liked him, she stopped willingly enough. 'I say, you may find this awful cheek, but I'm in a spot. I have to go over to Holland with Professor ter Laan-Luitinga, and it means leaving my wife for a week or ten days. She's expecting a baby and hates to be on her own, and none of her family or mine is free to go and stay with her. Sister Giles was complaining about being short of a nurse while you were on leave, and I wondered— if you hadn't anything better to do, if you would stay with Lottie?'

She had met his wife once, at Christmas when Mr Miles had brought her round the wards. They had liked each other, but they hadn't met since. Venetia said slowly, 'Well, I wasn't going anywhere—but how does your wife feel about it?'

'When I suggested it she was pleased. You have met, haven't you? I remember she liked you. Would you think about it? The professor will be going back to Holland in two or three days' time—he's got this tricky case to see to, and a backlog of patients to deal with. When do you start your holiday?'

Nothing in his manner suggested to her that he might already know.

'Well, I've days off on Monday and Tuesday, and then my holiday starts.'

'Couldn't be better, I believe we're to go on the Tuesday evening.'

He smiled in his friendly fashion. 'Leave a message at the lodge if you would like to come; we'd be eternally grateful.'

'If you're sure——?' began Venetia.

'Quite sure, and you've no idea what a load it would be off my mind.'

She thought about it for the rest of the day. It was a heaven-sent opportunity to get away from hospital life, and, when she came to think about it, hadn't someone told her that Mr Miles had bought a small cottage—somewhere near Beaconsfield? Penn, that was the name, and, although he and his wife had a small flat in one of the new blocks built by the Thames where the docks once were, they spent his free weekends and holidays there. She was a little surprised that he had asked her, but there probably wasn't anyone suitable free. By the end of the day she had made up her mind to accept his offer.

On the Friday evening he came on to the ward, very properly asked Sister Giles if he might have a word with Venetia, and drew her to one side.

'Lottie and I are so glad that you will come. She's at the flat, but if you could be ready to go with us on Tuesday afternoon, we'll collect you on the way down to the cottage at Penn; she would rather be there.'

He smiled kindly at her and went away, leaving her feeling pleasantly excited at the prospect of a change of scene.

She felt a little anxious as she waited for Mr Miles to fetch her; supposing his wife didn't like her after all? And what would they do all day? And would she be expected to help in the house? She wasn't really a guest, but, on the other hand, she wasn't employed by the Mileses, either.

She need not have worried; she was popped into the car, her luggage was stowed in the boot, and it was evident from the first moment that she and Mr Miles's wife were going to like each other.

'Call me Lottie,' begged the pretty girl sitting beside him, 'and I shall call you Venetia. You don't mind?'

It took a little while to leave London behind them, but once on the motorway they were going through Beaconsfield and turning off for Penn in no time at all. It was a charming village, just as Venetia had hoped it would be, with a green and a duck pond, surrounded by seventeenth-century cottages over-looked by the church and the Crown Inn. The Mileses' cottage was down a narrow lane, standing sideways on to the road; a small, neat house, its garden bare now, although very tidy. Inside there was a wel-coming fire in the sitting room, and an appetising smell coming from the kitchen.

'Mrs Trent,' explained Lottie. 'She comes in every day when we're here, just for an hour or two. Come and see your bedroom—we've only got two—Arthur will bring up your case.'

It was a dear little room, pink and blue and white, sparsely furnished, but there was everything one could need. 'We share the bathroom.' Lottie beamed at Venetia. 'I don't know what we'll do when baby gets here.'

Venetia peered out of the small window. 'Couldn't you build on? There's lots of room, isn't there? The garden's beautiful, and fairly big.'

'We don't want to leave here—we love it. Would you like to unpack? Arthur will have to go back almost at once...'

'Will you wish him a good trip from me? I'd like to unpack, if I may.'

It was obvious from her companion's face that she had said the right thing. She opened her case and started putting things away, and found that her thoughts, without any prompting from her, had turned to the professor. He would be going home—and to whom?

CHAPTER THREE

THE two of them settled down happily. They had a lot in common, for they were of a similar age and they both liked clothes, books and the theatre. Although Venetia had a small wardrobe, her clothes were as good as she could afford, even if not in the forefront of fashion. As for Lottie, a slavish follower of all fashion, but for the moment wearing voluminous garments which none the less contrived to look smart, she studied the latest *Harper's*, her pretty head full of the clothes she would buy when the baby was born.

Mrs Trent came daily to tidy the house and give what she called a good clean through, so Venetia and Lottie had a minimum of chores. They did the shopping, went for a walk each day, and spent the evenings round the fire, roasting chestnuts and knitting garments for the forthcoming infant. Each evening the phone rang, the signal for Venetia to go into the kitchen to start the supper while Lottie spent the next fifteen minutes or so talking to Arthur. It was on their fourth evening there that she remarked, putting down the phone at last, 'He doesn't know when he'll be back, he thinks at least another four days.'

Venetia came to the open door between the kitchen and the sitting-room. 'What exactly are they doing?' she wanted to know.

'Oh, some VIP needed brain surgery. Arthur doesn't always go with the professor, but now he's getting much more experienced—the professor's very generous with his teaching.' She looked up, smiling. 'He's a nice man. Do you see much of him at St Jude's?'

'Almost nothing, but he was very kind to me when my grandmother died.' Venetia began to beat the eggs for an omelette. 'He stitched up my arm, too.'

Lottie chuckled. 'I can just imagine the fuss and bother when they discovered that you were on the staff.'

Venetia spooned in water and did a bit more beating. 'Yes, it was funny, though I couldn't have cared less at the time.'

'A nasty experience. I'd have been terrified.'

'Well, I was, and I felt such a fool—I was sick while my arm was being stitched . . .'

'Not very glamorous, but then medical men expect that kind of thing,' observed Lottie comfortably.

But not very senior consultant surgeons who had descended from Olympian heights to do a bit of sewing on a student nurse's arm. But Venetia didn't say that out loud.

It was cold and wet the next day, and they spent it happily enough writing Christmas cards—not that Venetia had many to write, a lack more than made up for by the list Lottie worked her way through.

'Will you be in hospital over Christmas?' she wanted to know.

'Me? Oh, yes. It's quite fun, you know. We visit the other wards and sing carols, and each ward has a tree.'

'Could you have leave if you wanted it?'

Venetia said a little too quickly, 'Not really. We all get some time off, of course, but it's split up . . . Will you be here for Christmas?'

'Yes, Arthur's got the three days off. We'll go to his parents' on Christmas Eve, and mine on Boxing Day, but we'll have Christmas Day here together.'

'That's nice. That shop in the village has got some lovely tree decorations in. Do you want to buy some tomorrow?'

Christmas as a topic of conversation kept them busy until bedtime.

It was still cold the next morning, and the grey sky held a yellowish tinge. 'It's going to snow,' said Venetia as they walked briskly into the village and returned presently with a basket full of tinsel, baubles and the ingredients for a beef casserole.

'You ought to sort out the decorations,' suggested Venetia, 'while I get this casserole into a pot. I'll just nip into the garden and pull a couple of leeks.'

Easier said than done—there had been a hard frost for several nights and she had to prise them out with a gardening fork. The first few flakes of snow were falling as she went back indoors. A lovely wave of warm air met her as she opened the kitchen door, to stop short on the threshold and gape at the professor, who was leaning against the kitchen table, eating the carrots she had laid out neatly for the casserole.

'Come in and shut the door, Venetia. You're letting all the cold air in.'

She pushed the door shut with one foot and put the leeks beside the carrots. 'You're in Holland,' she said.

'An unnecessary remark, and untrue,' he pointed out. 'Arthur and I arrived here not ten minutes ago.'

'Oh, well, I'll go and——'

'No, you won't. They haven't seen each other for a week. Why do you think I am mewed up here with nothing but carrots to eat?'

She took off her coat and kicked off her boots. She looked small without them. She said tartly, 'You could get into that car of yours and drive home, and Mrs Todd would give you a super meal.'

'What an unkind girl you are, and what a way to talk to someone of my age! Besides, I've been invited to stay for lunch and tea. Will there be muffins?'

She could make neither head nor tail of him; she had thought of him as being reserved, taciturn almost, and certainly impatient, and at times positively unfriendly. She said weakly, 'Yes, we brought some muffins back from the village,' then added worriedly, 'but this casserole will never be ready for lunch. It'll have to be baked beans and eggs. I'll get this ready for this evening...'

'In that case, I'll stay for supper.' He stood up, his head only inches from the ceiling. 'Come, let's join the others.'

'I'm not very tidy...'

He studied her coolly. 'No, you aren't, but I don't think that matters.'

His voice was as cool as his look; it was the voice she was used to hearing at the hospital. Suddenly he had become the professor again, and not just a man eating carrots in the kitchen. She swept her hair away from her face. 'I was rude just now. I'm sorry. I wouldn't dare talk to you like that at St Jude's; I just forgot who you were for a moment.'

'I'm not sure if I'm flattered by that remark!' His alarming eyebrows rose in a mocking arc. He opened the door and swept her before him into the sitting-room.

Venetia went to bed that night in a state of pleasant bewilderment. The professor had stayed until late that evening, and he hadn't seemed like a professor at all—

he had washed up after their meals, buttered the muffins, eaten a splendid supper, and behaved as though he did all these things as a matter of course, whereas she was quite certain that in his own home he was neither called upon nor wished to perform such homely tasks.

More than that, he had fixed her with a compelling eye after lunch and suggested that she should accompany him on a walk. She had had her mouth open to refuse, and then realised that Arthur and Lottie might want to be alone. So she had fetched her coat and tied a scarf over her hair and gone walking with him. It had been very cold, and from time to time the snow had drifted down in a desultory fashion. After a few minutes, the professor had tucked her arm into his, shortening his great strides so that she could keep up. They had walked round the village green and the pond, and then taken one of the lanes leading from the village.

'Where does this go?' Venetia had asked.

'I haven't the faintest idea,' the professor had said, a remark to bring her to silence.

But the silence hadn't lasted long. He had begun to talk, and it wasn't until she was curled up in bed, remembering it all, that she realised she had told him a great deal more about herself than she had meant to. It was his voice, she decided. Sometimes it held a compelling tone which made it difficult to ignore. She supposed that students, on a teaching round with him and confronted by that cool, impersonal manner, might feel the same.

She decided sleepily that he hadn't known what to talk about, they had nothing in common. She forgot for the moment that they had shared delight in the wintry countryside around them, stopped to watch a squirrel foraging, a flight of rooks going home to their nests, paused for minutes to lean over a gate to watch a flock of sheep, and agreed that the country was a splendid place in which to live.

'You don't care for London and big cities?' he had asked casually.

'Well, I think perhaps the London I know isn't the same as yours. Some of the streets around St James's Park and that part of the world look delightful, and I suppose that if one lived there London might be very nice. But I love the country.' She had turned to face him. 'You can't be lonely there,' she had assured him earnestly.

They had played cards after supper, the four of them, and when Lottie had declared that she wanted a cup of tea before she went to bed the two men had gone into the kitchen to make it, which had given Venetia the chance to thank Lottie for her visit, and suggest that she caught the bus to Beaconsfield after breakfast and then a train back to town. She had supposed that Lottie would have agreed at once, since Arthur wasn't going back to St Jude's for two days, and she had been disconcerted when Lottie had told the men as they came from the kitchen. Arthur had said at once, 'Of course you'll stay, Venetia,' and the professor had put down the tray and stood looking at her.

'Venetia is spending the day with me tomorrow,' he had observed blandly.

'Me?' she had declared at once. 'Well, it's the first I've heard of it. Besides, I've a great many things to do. I don't know——'

'I'll be here at half-past nine,' the professor had continued just as though she hadn't spoken, and he had smiled at her with such kindness that she had nodded her head in what she now considered to be a very weak fashion.

'I should have said no,' she muttered, and went instantly to sleep.

The snow had ceased during the night, and it was a bright sunny morning with only a thin white blanket over the fields and hedges. The professor arrived at half-past nine exactly, and Venetia got into her coat, wishing that she had bought the new one she had promised herself, tied a scarf over her head once more, thrust her hands into woollen gloves, and pronounced herself ready. She spoke in her usual matter-of-fact manner, and evinced no excitement at the prospect of a day's outing with the professor, agreeing pleasantly that it was a splendid day for a drive, and at the same time wondering if the professor had invited her for the sole reason of taking her off the Mileses' hands. She wished suddenly that she had been firm about returning to St Jude's.

The professor stood watching her face, reading the expression upon it very accurately. He didn't allow her more than a few minutes in which to say a temporary goodbye, but propelled her gently out into the car, helped her in and got in beside her. For all the aloofness of his manner, he was good at putting his patients at their ease. He applied himself to doing just that with Venetia. He embarked on a gentle flow of talk and watched her relax, and only then did he say casually, 'I thought we might go to the sea, somewhere along the south coast. There's a pleasant village—Findon—just inland from Worthing. We might lunch there and then go for a walk by the sea. Would you like that?'

'Oh, yes. I would.' Her lovely eyes sparkled and she went a little pink at the thought of it.

'You go to the sea often?'

'Well, no. I—I always spent my holidays with Granny. She liked going to art galleries and museums, and sometimes we had a day out—you know, to Windsor or Henley—she loved the Thames, and once we went to the village where she used to live.'

She stopped. 'I'm sorry, I must be boring you.'

'No. We are an unlikely pair, are we not, Venetia? And yet we contrive to suit each other very well.'

She thought his remark over very carefully, but even if she could have thought of a suitable reply he didn't give her the chance, but slowed the car and stopped outside a country pub. 'Coffee? This looks all right.'

It was when they were in the car once again, going towards the coast, that he began to tell her something of himself.

'I have a ward,' he confided. 'A friend of mine died several years ago, and I discovered that I was her guardian. She is at a finishing school in Switzerland, but she returns for Christmas—this is her last term. When she is eighteen she is to go to an aunt in America, but until then she will live with me.'

'You're not married?'

'No. Not yet. I have never found a woman I would want to make my wife, and I suspect that I am getting too old now.'

'Rubbish!' said Venetia strongly, quite forgetting that he was a professor and entitled to respect from a mere student nurse. 'You're not a bit old.'

'Thirty-five.'

She hoped that he might go on talking about himself, but she was to be disappointed; he talked about everything else under the sun for the rest of the day, but never another word of a personal nature.

They reached Findon in good time for lunch, and stopped in the square at Darling's Bistro, a cosy, small restaurant where they ate Stilton pâté with pears, raised turkey pie, and rounded off their meal with a lemon-and-lime soufflé and all the coffee they could drink. Venetia ate with a healthy appetite, watched with an appreciative gleam by her companion, and when he suggested that they might drive on to the coast and take a walk by the sea, she agreed that they should like a happy child.

She didn't ask where they were going, she was content to wait and see. He drove to Brighton, where he parked the car and walked her for miles along the promenade, until her cheeks glowed and her eyes sparkled. Back in the town they had tea in the Lanes and spent half an hour looking in the shop windows there. There was a lot to see—antiques, jewellers, expensive boutiques—but dusk was already upon them as the red sun sank. The professor stowed her in the car once more and drove back along the coast road, talking of this and that until they were going through Ascot. It was dark by now, and the thin coating of snow, glistening with frost, glittered in the car's powerful headlights.

'I thought we might have dinner. There's a nice place at Sonning, the White Hart.'

'Thank you, Professor, but shouldn't I be getting back? Won't we be expected?'

'No. I think that if we get back by ten o'clock that will be just about right. They don't see all that much of each other, you know. I work Arthur pretty hard.'

'Oh, of course. How silly of me not to think of that. But don't you want to go home?'

The professor smiled thinly in the dark. 'Not before I've had my dinner. But perhaps you feel you've had enough of my company?' His voice was silky.

She turned to look at him through the gloom. 'Good heavens, no, Professor, I'm having a lovely time.' She was silent for a moment. 'But I think I'm not the usual kind of girl you take out, am I? And you've been more than kind.'

'I am relieved, Venetia. I was wondering if I bored you.'

'Well, what a silly idea!' she said roundly. 'I don't suppose you've bored anyone in your life. I have always thought that you were...' she paused to find the right word '...detached. No, that's not the right word—I think I mean disinterested, or do I mean indifferent? Anyway, all the nurses are scared of you, but at the same time they admire you tremendously. You see, you're a mystery. You come and go and no one knows anything about you, whereas we all know that Mr Wells has three children and a wife who was a nurse, and Mr Farr is a grandfather, and Dr Tomkinson has just got engaged——'

'I perceive that there is no privacy in the hospital.'

'Well, not much,' said Venetia matter-of-factly. 'There's always gossip, but it's mostly good-natured. You know who's going out with whom.'

'You mean the nursing staff and young doctors, I presume.'

'Yes—some of the nurses are awfully pretty...'

'And you, Venetia? Do you go out with the young doctors?'

'Me? No, of course not. I'm not pretty, and I'm not smart. Besides, I've always had Granny.'

He said blandly, 'I am greatly enlightened, I must do my utmost not to frighten the nurses. Do I frighten you, Venetia?'

'Gracious, no. Well, not frighten exactly. I was just a bit in awe of you, perhaps, but not now.'

'I'm glad to hear that. So we are able to dine together in a friendly fashion?'

'I'd like to, thank you. Only do remember that I'm not dressed for anywhere smart.'

The professor's firm mouth twitched into a smile. 'The place I have in mind will suit us both, I believe.'

The hotel looked welcoming, and once inside Venetia went away to do her face and comb her hair. The result hardly satisfied her, but no amount of looking into the mirror was going to improve matters. She joined the professor in the bar, and drank her sherry and made polite small talk, conscious that compared with the other girls there she looked dowdy.

She didn't allow it to spoil her evening, though. Sitting at a table opposite the professor, she perused the menu, trying to make up her mind what to have. Everything was frightfully expensive and she frowned, looking for a reasonably priced dish. The professor, watching her with well-concealed amusement, took pity on her.

'What about pheasant in red wine and chestnuts?' he wanted to know, with just the right amount of casualness, 'and perhaps smoked salmon and prawn salad to start with?'

She agreed with relief, and when the food came ate it with pleasure. A refreshing change, mused the professor, urging her to have some more scalloped potatoes, remembering the young women he had dined with who had nibbled at celery sticks and only eaten things when they were out of season. The shortbread meringue gâteau, when it came, was a miracle of pastry, meringue, fresh apricots and lashings of whipped cream. Venetia had two helpings, and told him that it was just the most delicious dessert she had ever eaten. 'Not,' she added thoughtfully, 'that I've eaten a great many! The food at St Jude's is wholesome, but most of the time we have to eat fast, so long as it's food it doesn't really matter what it is, if you see what I mean.'

The professor agreed that he saw just what she meant, and ordered coffee. He was surprised that he was enjoying himself more than he had done for a long time.

They got back to Penn just after ten o'clock, and sat talking for half an hour before the professor got up to go. Venetia, half-way through a thank you speech, was ruthlessly cut short. 'I must find a Christmas present for my ward,' he told her. 'I hope you will come with me tomorrow and help me—I have not the least idea ...'

'Oh, what a good idea,' said Lottie before Venetia could speak. 'Where will you go?'

'I thought the Cotswolds; a good hunting-ground for the kind of thing she likes—small antiques, jewellery perhaps.' He glanced at Venetia, who still hadn't spoken. 'Half-past nine?' He made the question sound like a statement not to be gainsaid.

She heard herself meekly agreeing, although she had meant to refuse.

It was a lovely morning again. She wished that she had something different to wear as she got into her plain jersey dress and winter coat—even her shoes were sensible ... She went downstairs and found the professor in the kitchen, talking to the Mileses who were washing up together.

His 'Good morning, Venetia,' was brisk, and he wasted no time in trivial conversation. She found herself in the car and being driven away before she could say more than a brief goodbye to Lottie.

She said with a touch of peevishness, 'I'm going back to St Jude's tomorrow.'

'So am I—I'll give you a lift. Arthur won't need to come in until the afternoon. I've a list then.'

'I can get a bus!'

He took no notice of this. 'About eleven o'clock suit you?' he wanted to know, and he didn't wait for her answer. 'I think it will snow before tomorrow. It looks as though we shall have a white Christmas. There'll be skating on the canals.'

'You will go to Holland?'

'Oh, yes. At the end of the week; I want to be at home when Anneta gets back.'

Venetia was conscious of a feeling of disappointment, and dismissed it at once as absurd. After all, if she saw the professor once in a week it was unusual, and if and when they did come across each other he quite often gave her a cool stare.

They stopped for coffee once he had circumnavigated Oxford, and then drove on to Cirencester to turn north then through Fossebridge and Bourton-on-the-Water to stop in Moreton-in-Marsh.

'A happy hunting-ground for antiques,' explained the professor, 'and as good a place as any for lunch.'

The hotel was in the main street, a nice old house with a comfortable dining-room and a small, cosy bar. They ate roast partridge with crunchy stuffing balls, fried bread and french beans, and followed these with a chocolate chestnut gâteau. They drank white wine, but since the professor was driving he had only one glass. They didn't linger long over coffee, but began a brisk walk along the wide main street, stopping to look in any likely shop windows.

'That's nice,' observed Venetia, peering into a small window crammed with antique jewellery and charming bric-a-brac. She pointed to a delicate gold necklace, studded at intervals with small pearls, and with a pearl pendant encircling a peridot from which in turn were suspended more pearls with an oval peridot at their end. It was a fragile thing, and just right for a young girl. 'And it would look lovely with any colouring, dark or fair.'

'Then we will buy it.' She was marched into the dim interior and spent a delightful five minutes while the professor made his purchase. He joined her presently and asked carelessly, 'Does anything take your fancy?'

'Almost everything. But if you hadn't bought the pendant I think she might have liked this, too.' She pointed to a necklet of amethysts, interspersed with green enamel leaves set with tiny pearls.

'I think the pendant is more her sort of thing, but this is charming.'

The owner joined them, an old man who smiled at them and told them to look their fill. 'A charming piece,' he added. 'Early nineteenth-century. It comes from a local family, and was made to an ancestor's design for his bride. It is said that she was a shy girl, and very gentle, and the amethysts were the nearest he could get to the colour of a violet, for that is how he thought of her.'

'What a sweet story,' said Venetia. 'And how the family must have hated to part with it.'

'The family has died out, unfortunately; the estate was sold and everything with it. I like to think that whoever buys it and wears it will remember its story.'

They went presently, to peer into other shop windows and then return to the car. The short day was losing its light and they were a long way from Penn.

'We'll stop in Woodstock for tea,' remarked the professor, getting into the car beside her.

It was dark when they stopped again outside the Bear Inn, and it was lovely to go into the lighted rooms with their big fires. They had tea and muffins and talked idly, arguing occasionally in a friendly way, and laughing, too, but back in the car, sitting silent beside the professor's great bulk, Venetia worried. It really would not do, she reflected. They had slipped into an easy friendship which was quite at variance with their allotted spheres. After today, she told herself, she would take care to avoid him. And possibly, once back at St Jude's, he would avoid her—not intentionally, but for the simple reason that she would be one of dozens of student nurses who really had nothing to do with his own life, but were there to do his bidding and listen to his lectures.

She gave a small sigh of satisfaction at having settled the matter, and the professor said, 'I think we'd better take pity on Arthur and Lottie again, don't you? Do you like Italian food?'

'Pizzas?' She shook her head. 'No, not really.'

'Not pizza.' He smiled to himself. 'It's time you sampled lasagne properly made. There's a place in Beaconsfield—Santella's—and don't worry, I'll get you back to the cottage by ten o'clock. I dare say you'll want to pack.'

She opened her mouth to refuse, and then decided not to. After all, she wasn't likely to be asked out to dinner again in a hurry. 'Thank you,' she said. 'It sounds very nice.'

She agreed that lasagne was not in the least like a pizza. Indeed, she liked it very much. She had enjoyed the carrot and coriander soup which had preceded it, too, and rounded off the meal with a lavish ice-cream which, as the professor pointed out, it was impossible to forgo since the restaurant was Italian, and the Italians were famous for their ices.

True to his word, he took her back well before ten o'clock, and this time he didn't stay, only reiterated that he would fetch her at eleven o'clock the next morning and she was to mind that she was ready.

She stayed a little while talking to Lottie and Arthur after he had gone, and then went to her bed, tired but deeply content. It was only when she awakened in the night and remembered that she would be back on the ward in another day's time, and wouldn't see the professor—not to talk to, anyway—again, and that he was going back to Holland very shortly, that her contentment gave way to a feeling of loneliness, so strong that she was forced to tell herself not to give way to self-pity.

By the time they had had breakfast and she had packed her case the professor was at the door, and it seemed to her, her farewells said and herself in the car beside him once more, that he was already distancing himself from her. He had little to say other than a civil enquiry as to whether she had slept well, and the observation that it seemed likely to snow again, and there was no loitering on the way, either.

He parked the car outside the entrance and got out to open her door and get her case from the boot, but when she put her hand out for it he ignored it, and carried the case through the doors and across the entrance hall to where the door to the nurses' home was. He put it down then, and stood looking down at her, and it saddened her to see the look on his face: impersonal, almost indifferent. All the same, she put out a hand and said quietly, 'Thank you very much, Professor. I—enjoyed all that driving, it was very kind of you.'

He took her hand in his large firm one and held it briefly. All he said was, 'You needed a holiday.' He opened the door for her, and she picked up her case and went through it into the long, dark passage to the nurses' quarters. She didn't look back, and before she was half-way there she heard the door close.

It was a good thing the ward was busy when she went on duty the next morning, for she had no time to think about anything other than her work. Staff Nurse Thomas was in a sour mood, too, chivvying her to and fro, finding fault and complaining that she wasn't going to make a good nurse, not in a month of Sundays. The patients were nice, though. There were several convalescents, busy making Christmas decorations, and those who were too ill to do anything grinned cheerfully and called weakly across the ward to each other, arguing about football and the pools. Venetia nipped to and fro and, whenever she had a moment, stopped to fill in a coupon for someone too ill to hold a pen. Each time the ward door opened she looked round, wishing and at the same time not wishing to see the professor, but he didn't come. There was no reason for him to do so; there were no head injuries needing his attention.

There was no sign of him all day, although one of the theatre staff held forth at length over dinner, giving a blow by blow account of a four-hour operation he had done that morning.

'He's gorgeous,' she enthused. 'Never loses his cool, and never shouts like some I could mention. We'll all miss him . . .'

She got up to fetch her pudding and stopped to talk to someone at another table, so Venetia, with not another minute to spare before going back on duty, never discovered why he would be missed. Surely he wasn't leaving forever? He had said he was going home for Christmas, but that could mean anything. She loitered along the corridors thinking about it, and got back three minutes late, to Staff Nurse Thomas's nagging reproaches.

She saw him the next day. He was coming towards her across the entrance hall where she had gone to fetch something for Sister from the lodge. He had Mr Miles with him and two housemen and, although Arthur smiled at her, the professor merely gave her a cold stare. And that same evening she heard that he had gone back to Holland.

Christmas was almost upon them. The ward had to be decorated; such patients who were able to go had to be discharged, some to return once Christmas was over; the remainder were rearranged so that the ill ones were at one end of the ward in comparative peace and quiet; and, since it was the festive season which brought the inevitable accidents with it, beds were made up in readiness for the expected casualties. Sure enough, in they came, mostly with stab wounds, jagged cuts from broken bottles, and slashed hands and arms, and along with them came a sprinkling of appendixes, gall bladders and gastric ulcers. Venetia was too tired to do much more than go to bed when she got off duty, although she went to several parties in the hospital. Although none of the young doctors found her attractive, they liked her because she was

kind and listened when they talked to her. They tended
to ask her advice about their love-affairs, too, and she
never lacked for someone to talk to. All the same, she
was glad when Christmas was over, even though the
round of parties and extra work on the wards had
given rise to short tempers and a good deal of
peevishness. Even Sister Giles was irritable, and Staff
Nurse Thomas was in a continuous rage about something or other.

Venetia, on the way to the dispensary with a rude
message from that lady about the non-sending of a
drug she had ordered, was glad to get away from the
ward for a few minutes. She took the long way round
in order to spin out her freedom, and didn't hurry,
so the professor, who was following her, had no difficulty in catching up with her as she went past the
boiler-room and slowed her steps to call a cheerful
good morning to the engineer there.

'And good morning to you, too, Venetia,' said the
professor in her ear. She whirled round so quickly
that he put out an arm to steady her.

'Good morning, sir. You made me jump.' She re-
treated a little from him and started walking again,
and this time he stayed with her. His voice, cool and
so authoritative, halted her again. 'I wish to talk to
you, Nurse. When are you free?'

'I'm on duty all day, sir.'

'In that case I will come to the ward.'

She forgot whom she was talking to for a moment.
'Oh, you can't do that...'

He turned his dark eyes on her, his eyebrows raised
in cold astonishment. 'I can do as I wish, Nurse. I
will see you later.'

He turned on his heel and walked unhurriedly away,
and the engineer, who had been shamelessly eaves-

dropping, said, 'Cor, Nurse! What've you been up to?'

A question which she pondered for the rest of the morning; it took away her appetite at dinner. But perhaps he wouldn't come...

CHAPTER FOUR

THE professor came half-way through the afternoon, stalking through the ward to Sister's office. Venetia, explaining to an irate Staff Nurse Thomas just why she had gone to fetch old Mr Pike a drink when she was supposed to be taking his temperature, peeped through a gap in the cubicle curtains and her heart sank, for he looked to be at his most formidable. Allowing her senior's diatribe to flow over her head, she searched her mind for any awful mistakes she might have made, but none came to mind worthy of his august wrath. Besides, she reminded herself hopefully, he had his own department and theatre in the hospital, and she had had nothing to do with any of his patients.

Her unhappy musings were brought to a halt by the arrival of Sister Giles, requesting her to go to her office where Professor ter Laan-Luitinga was waiting. She gave Venetia an encouraging smile as she spoke, but Venetia still paused by the door before she knocked, and in answer to his 'Come' went in.

He was standing at the window, staring out, his back to her, but when she closed the door behind her he turned round. Since he didn't speak, and the silence became rather more than she could bear, she said woodenly, 'You wanted to see me, sir?'

He drew forward the small wooden chair facing Sister's desk. 'Do sit down. You are wondering why I wish to speak to you?'

'Well, yes, I am rather...'

He sat down on the side of the desk, uncaring of the neat stacks of charts and forms waiting for Sister Giles's attention. He didn't speak for a minute or more, and Venetia, sitting very still, her hands folded on her aproned lap, wished very much to jump up and rush from the room. Instead she clutched her hands together very tightly and fixed her eyes on the professor's waistcoat.

'I have been home, as you know,' he said finally, 'and I have had time to reflect. I have given the matter considerable thought, and it seems to me that it would be to our mutual advantage if you were to become my wife.'

Venetia goggled at him. 'Your wife?' and then, 'Your wife? You must be joking...'

She saw his eyebrows come together in a heavy frown and went on hastily, 'No, all right, you're not joking, only it's so—so unexpected.' And since he remained silent, 'What I mean is—it doesn't seem a very good idea. I'm quite sure that you aren't—that is...' she paused, took a breath and went on, rather pink in the face '... I don't think I'm the kind of girl you would fall in love with, and I've never had the least...' She fell silent. Really, she thought crossly, a girl shouldn't have to explain the matter to a man who had just proposed to her.

'You are labouring under a misapprehension,' he observed impatiently. 'I have not mentioned falling in love to you, only that you would make me a suitable wife.' Venetia opened her mouth to utter and he went on testily, 'No, don't keep interrupting. Allow me to explain. You remember that I have a ward, a girl of seventeen, left in my charge by a lifelong friend who died some years ago? She has just left her school in Switzerland, and will live at home with me until she is eighteen, when she is to go to her aunt who lives in the States. Until now I have seen very little of her—there has been a companion at my home who looked after her during her holidays, but this lady has retired. I am unable to remain at home for any length of time because of my work, and in any case I believe that I am unsuitable for the task of looking after my ward. She has recently become rather wayward in her life-style, so the school authorities tell me, and she needs someone to check her until such time as I can relinquish my guardianship and hand her over to her aunt. I have no family living within a reasonable distance of my home, and it occurs to me that a sensible girl such as yourself, with no ties, could take my ward in charge, entertain my friends and run my household.'

Venetia's eyes were like saucers. 'How about a governess or a housekeeper? I should have thought either one or both would be sensible . . . ?'

She sensed his impatience. 'No, Anneta needs a secure, affectionate family background; she also needs someone young enough for her to confide in and who will understand her. At the same time she needs a level-headed parent to guide her—give her an example of a contented, harmonious marriage. In fact, I understand that some of her friends come from homes where divorce is more the rule than the exception.'

'And us? You and me?' said Venetia. 'Will we be contented and harmonious?' She looked around the rather dreary little office wildly. 'And what about when she goes to this aunt in America? Quite likely by then we shan't be either of these things.'

'A matter we are surely sensible enough to settle between us when the time comes. I assure you that you will be provided for if you should choose to terminate our marriage.'

'Why me?'

'Have I not made myself clear? You are exactly the kind of young woman Anneta is most likely to listen to. You have no family, no home and no prospect of marrying. I am offering you these things in return, and all I ask is for you to be a guiding light to her, a hostess to my guests, and to fulfil the role of wife and mistress of my home. I think and hope that we may be more than friends in time, but until then we shall remain just that—friends.'

He smiled suddenly, and just for a moment she glimpsed a quite different man behind his reserve. She said hesitantly, 'You're sure you're not in love with anyone? It would be awful if you married me and fell in love with someone else.'

'The thought had crossed my mind, but I am no longer in my first youth, and I have had my fill of falling in love. I lead a busy life, and my work absorbs my days.' He got up and walked to the window, peered out and turned his back on the depressing view. 'But I have a great many friends, and you would not find your life dull. Besides, there will be Anneta.'

'You really mean it?'

He became all at once aloof. 'My dear girl, do you suppose that I would waste your time on a pointless discussion? Or mine, for that matter? Of course, I mean it.'

She studied his face. She liked him, there was no denying that, but she was rather in awe of him, too. She might make the most frightful mess of marrying him, and the bit about being a hostess to his friends was rather intimidating. Anneta, too, was going to be a handful. On the other hand, what did the future hold for her? Very little, as far as she could see. A safe job, to be sure, if she passed her finals, and after that? Years of hospital wards and, if she was lucky enough, a ward sister's post. The professor was right when he had pointed out that she had no prospects regarding marriage. No one, so far, had ever asked her to marry him, and she thought it unlikely that anyone would. But the professor had...

'My mind is confused. May I think about it?' she asked him.

'Certainly. Are you free tomorrow evening? Yes? Good. I will be outside at half-past six. We will go home and you may give your answer then.'

She got to her feet. Sister Giles would be hopping mad by now, and Staff Nurse Thomas would be gibbering with rage. 'I'd better go...' She sounded anxious without knowing it, and he went to the door with her. He paused with his hand on it, towering over her, smiling so kindly that she blinked and felt a little rush of warm feeling under her ribs.

'I'll come with you,' he told her.

He had a great deal of authority, although he seldom showed it; his few words of explanation had the effect of silencing any remarks Staff Nurse Thomas had been bottling up, and Sister Giles, beyond requesting her to get on with her work as quickly as possible, had nothing to say. Only Staff Nurse Thomas, as they were going to their dinners, muttered, 'Gave you a good telling off, did he? You'd better look out, Nurse Forbes, or you'll find yourself looking for another way of life.'

Venetia forbore to tell her that she didn't need to look, it had been offered to her.

She spent the rest of the day vacillating between agreeing to the professor's proposal and turning it down flat. Indeed, she rehearsed a number of suitable and dignified speeches in which she thanked him nicely for his offer and explained why it would be impossible for her to accept it. She was vague as to her reasons for refusing, and the possibility of his querying them was something she ignored. She still wasn't quite sure that he had actually meant what he had said. On the other hand, from time to time, when Staff Nurse Thomas was particularly nasty, she viewed the idea of marriage to the professor as decidedly the lesser of two evils. She went to bed with her head in a splendid muddle, sure that she would lie awake and worry all night. She went to sleep the moment her head touched the pillow.

Since it was take-in week there was no opportunity to give the matter further thought during the following day. Tired out after a day of being at her senior's beck and call, and with her insides rumbling in protest at hurried meals snatched when a few minutes could be spared, she went off duty half an hour later, her one desire to have her supper and go to bed after a lengthy bath. If she had known how to get hold of the professor and back out of their evening together she would have done so, but she hadn't seen him all day, and she balked at asking anyone. There was nothing for it but to shower and change and go and meet him. At least she was sure that she would have a lovely supper. She only hoped she wouldn't drop off over it . . .

It was, she felt, a special occasion, and merited a certain amount of extra care with her appearance. There was a wool dress at the back of her wardrobe; it had been expensive when she had bought it at least two years ago, and it had been chosen with the intention of wearing it for years to come. It was grey, a useful colour, she had considered at the time, but it had never suited her, and now it did even less than that. She peered at her reflection without enthusiasm, brushed her hair from its tidy chignon and allowed it to frame her face, powdered her pale face and put on lipstick. Surely the professor would change his mind when she appeared? A more unsuitable candidate for the honour of being a well-known surgeon's wife would surely be hard to find? She got into her coat, stuck her feet into her only pair of court shoes, and went down to the front entrance.

The professor was standing just inside the doors, talking to Arthur Miles. He watched Venetia coming towards them, appraising her appearance with a knowledgeable eye. Neat and unspectacular, he decided, listening with half an ear to his companion. She would repay dressing, and she had a pleasantly unselfconscious air about her. She would be entirely suitable as his wife; she was undemanding and intelligent and a good companion—indeed, he had enjoyed her companionship, aware that there was nothing about her to distract him from his work. And she would be good for Anneta, who was proving to be a problem which was beyond the powers of even the most brilliant of surgeons...

He said briefly, 'Here's Venetia,' and went to meet her with Arthur beside him. They talked for a few minutes—about Lottie and the cottage—and presently Arthur went away and they went out to the car. The professor had nothing much to say as he drove to Hampstead, and Venetia was far too occupied rehearsing her speech to notice.

Todd opened the door to them and Mrs Todd took her away to tidy herself before she joined the professor in his drawing-room. The cat was sitting before the fire and Venetia, glad of a topic of conversation, said, 'Oh, hello. Does she belong to you?'

The professor got up and ushered her to a chair near the fire. 'Orthia—let us say rather that she attached herself to my household some months ago under the impression that we belong to her.'

Venetia thought for a moment. 'A Greek name, isn't it?'

'Yes—or if you prefer Artemis or Diana...'

'She hunts.' Venetia bent to stroke the furry head. 'This cat looks much too cosy to do more than drink a saucer of milk.'

He got up to pour her a drink and then began a gentle conversation which required very little effort on her part, and presently Todd came to announce that dinner was ready, and they crossed the hall to the dining-room. She hadn't been in it before; it was elegantly furnished and softly lit and the table gleamed with silver and crystal. As she took her seat opposite her host she reflected that it wasn't quite fair to eat a splendid dinner under false pretences, for she could so easily have told him that she had made up her mind to refuse him. This thought was expunged by the sensible one that, since she was here, she might as well enjoy the delicious food which was offered to her.

And it was delicious; Tarte Valentinoise followed by grilled trout with pepper sauce, *rissole* potatoes, braised chicory and a purée of carrots. They drank a white wine, but when Todd had served a chestnut soufflé he set fresh glasses on the table and opened a bottle of champagne.

Venetia, who had enjoyed every morsel and carried on quite successful small talk while doing so, had a sudden suspicious thought as the cork popped, but the professor's face was, as usual, bland and slightly withdrawn, and he continued to talk about the books they had been discussing. Only when the champagne had been poured did he say casually, 'A toast to you, Venetia, either in celebration of our engagement or a means by which I may drown my disappointment.'

It hadn't been at all what she had expected; it was almost as though he had anticipated her refusal. Her reaction was very feminine and exactly what he had expected it to be. 'Well, I haven't said anything yet...'

It was a chance to embark on her prepared speech, only she wasn't given the chance to do so. 'You like champagne?'

'Well, I don't know.' She took a sip, and then another. 'It's rather nice,' she observed, 'but it's not very strong, is it? I thought it made you feel up in the clouds.'

The professor hid a smile. 'Drink up and have another glass,' he said. 'I think it is more accurate to say that it gives one a feeling of elation.'

Venetia thought that she felt just the same as usual as they went back to the drawing-room for their coffee. True, she turned a kindlier eye upon her host as she handed him his coffee—she even felt prepared to offer some advice as to whom he might marry since she was about to refuse him.

She drank her coffee, and when Orthia jumped on to her lap she sat comfortably, stroking the furry head. She took a breath and began, 'Thank you for inviting me to dinner. It was lovely...' she paused for a moment to contemplate in retrospect the perfection of the chestnut soufflé '...but I think I should tell you that I must refuse your—your offer.'

'Why?' He sounded mildly interested, no more.

'Well...' She came to a halt simply because her head was empty of a single reason for refusing him. 'I'm not suitable,' she began.

'You said that yesterday. You will allow me to know whom I consider suitable to be my wife.'

If anybody else had said that she would have accused him of arrogance and pomposity, but somehow it didn't sound like either of these things when the professor uttered it. She had the impression that he really did know best, and if she agreed to marry him she would fulfil all his ideas of suitability. All the same, she tried again. 'I don't think that I believe that two people should marry unless they—they love each other.'

'A sound sentiment, but there are variations of love, Venetia. Would our marriage be less likely to prosper because we are not in love, compared with a couple who have a fleeting infatuation for each other and, on the crest of it, marry only to find that they have nothing in common—no shared interests, no pleasure in each other's company, no wish to make the marriage work?' He smiled suddenly. 'I'm sorry if I should sound prosy.'

She shook her head. 'You make it sound sensible. But what about us? Do we have shared interests and—and pleasure in each other's company?'

'Oh, yes. I enjoy your company, and I believe that you enjoy mine, and you have been at the hospital long enough to understand my work and bear with me when I come home full of grumbles after a bad day.' He added bracingly, 'Besides, we shall see very little of each other; I have a full appointment book for the next month or so.'

He fell silent and she realised that she would have to give him his answer. A faint feeling of irritation swelled her bosom; there he sat, looking for all the world as though nothing mattered, and even if it did he would be too lazy to do anything about it, while she had to make the most difficult decision of her life. She would refuse him, once and for all ...

'Well?' It was amazing how just one word could convey a sense of comfort and assurance.

Her tongue took over from her with a life of its own. She heard herself agreeing to marry him in a voice which held no doubts.

'Thank you, Venetia,' he said gravely. 'I believe that we shall deal very well together. Two lonely people with good reasons for marrying.'

'Yes, well, I hope so, too. I was going to refuse you, you know.'

'Yes. I knew.' He smiled again, very kindly so that she smiled back. 'Do you feel like making some plans while you are here? I am going back to Holland in eight days' time, and I should like to take you with me as my wife.' When she opened her mouth to speak, 'No, don't interrupt—I can arrange for you to leave the hospital in a couple of days' time. Lottie will love to have you. I'll get a special licence and we can be married quietly. Anneta is staying with friends until I go back home. Naturally, she doesn't know about us, and I don't intend to tell her.'

Venetia took time off from a contemplation of the married state to wonder if this was wise. She asked worriedly, 'Will she mind?'

She had a glimpse of the professor at his most impassive. 'Probably, but since our marriage will be a *fait accompli* there is little that she can do about it.'

Except make life difficult for everyone, thought Venetia, but wisely held her tongue and was rewarded by his, 'I think that the two of us will be able to overcome any slight disturbance.' He added smoothly, 'If you should have second thoughts, I shall understand.'

'I said I would marry you,' declared Venetia matter-of-factly, 'and I will.' She twiddled one of Orthia's ears and didn't look at him. 'I only hope that I'll be a good hostess, for I have no idea of how to set about it.'

'Just be yourself. I think you may find it easier than working on the wards.'

She gave him a clear, honest look. 'I shall do my best. Thank you for asking me to be your wife, Professor.'

'It is I who thanks you, Venetia. My name is Duert, by the way.'

'Oh, is it? It's a nice name. Would you mind if I went back now? I'm on duty at seven-thirty tomorrow. How will I know...?'

'I'll see that you are kept informed. Leave everything to me, Venetia.'

She got to her feet and they walked together into the hall, where Todd appeared silently with her coat.

'Miss Forbes and I would like you and Mrs Todd to know that we shall be marrying shortly, Todd.'

Todd beamed. 'Well, now, sir and Miss Forbes, that is a splendid piece of news. Mrs Todd will be that pleased.'

The professor thanked him and Venetia murmured suitably; any moment now, she was beginning to feel, she would wake up and find the whole business a dream.

They spoke little on the way back to St Jude's, and at the entrance the professor got out, helped her from the car and went in with her. He walked to the door leading to the nurses' home and stood looking down at her.

'Sleep soundly, my dear.' He picked up one of her hands and kissed it gently. 'Goodnight.'

She whispered goodnight and went past him and heard him shut the door behind her. The sound was final and she said out loud. 'My goodness, why have I said yes when I meant no? But I won't back out...'

She went up to her room, and since it was late none of her friends were about, so she was able to creep along to a bathroom and then tumble into bed, to sleep as soundly as the professor had wished her to.

She told none of her friends of her future plans as they gobbled down their breakfast—time enough for that when she heard from the professor. The morning went by with Staff Nurse Thomas breathing down her neck at every turn, so she became clumsy and nervous and not at all her usual self. After dinner she became even more jumpy when a patient was admitted with head injuries and Arthur Miles came on to the ward and, presently, the professor. He walked past her as though she hadn't been there, two housemen trailing him and Sister Giles hurrying over to meet him, and Venetia, who just for the moment had the absurd idea that he might smile at her at least, dropped a pair of forceps which she was handing to Staff Nurse Thomas and got soundly rated for it.

He went back through the ward when he had finished his examination, but she took care to be bending over a patient and didn't look up—at least, not until he had reached the door. Even from the back he looked remote, unapproachable... He turned his head and looked at her down the length of the ward; there was no expression on his face, only a faint indifference.

Ten minutes later she was sent for to go to the office. 'And what have you done this time?' asked Staff Nurse Thomas nastily.

Venetia knocked on the office door, wishing for support of some sort—physical or moral, either would do. Miss Hawkins was of the old-fashioned school, and, from her point of view, the nursing profession hadn't changed one iota since she herself had trained decades earlier. That this point of view led to a good deal of acrimony between herself and authority made no difference, for she would retire in a year's time, and until then she kept to her own ideas—sound ones, but a touch severe, so that the junior nurses were unwillingly in awe of her.

She sat behind her desk now, its contents tidily arranged before her, her old-fashioned cap erect on her severely dressed hair, her majestic bosom encased in blue serge. She was not alone; here was the support Venetia craved, the professor, sitting at his ease near the desk.

'Come in, Nurse Forbes. Sit down.' She watched while he got up, offered his chair to Venetia and took another one for himself. 'Professor ter Laan-Luitinga tells me that you are to be married, and has asked for your release from your contract since he is desirous of taking you back to Holland as his wife. The circumstances are unusual, but since he has already spoken to the board of governors, I am happy to add my consent to theirs.'

She made it sound as though any decision of theirs would have been useless without her endorsement, and the professor's eyes gleamed with amusement.

'Venetia and I are most grateful to you, Miss Hawkins. I take it that she may leave as soon as she can pack her things? She will be going to stay with Mrs Miles until the wedding.'

'Ah, yes, Mrs Miles. Such a good nurse—excellent sister material, a pity she married.' She smiled at the professor, one of the few people she respected and liked as well, then modified the smile for Venetia's benefit, wished them happy, and bowed her head graciously in dismissal.

Outside the door Venetia said warmly, 'Thank you for being there—we're all a bit scared of her, you know.'

'Yes, I know. I thought it might help.'

'You looked right through me just now on the ward,' she told him severely.

'Well, of course I did. Where are your wits, Venetia? I imagine that you will shortly be the object of more gossip than you would like. I don't intend to add to it.'

'Oh, I hadn't thought of that.' She edged by him. 'I must go back to the ward.'

'I imagine that you must work for the rest of the day, but tomorrow you should be free to pack your things. I will be outside at half-past six tomorrow evening. Lottie expects you.' He turned away and then halted.

'I have arranged for us to be married in a week's time.'

She forgot her urgency to return to the ward. 'Well, really, don't you know that the bride decides the date? I've no clothes, for a start.'

'You may buy all the clothes you want in Holland. But surely you can find something fit to wear before then?'

She seethed. 'You mean that I have nothing fit to wear? You are the rudest man!'

'I have no intention of annoying you, Venetia. Please do your best to be ready in a week's time. If you need money, you have only to say so. I have a backlog of work, so it is unlikely that we shall see much of each other until then, but I will let you know the church and the time within the next day or so.'

Sheer misery welled up inside her; what a way in which to start married life, although in all honesty she had to admit that to behave otherwise would have been a hollow sham. She said woodenly, 'I have enough money, thank you, and I'll be ready when you say so.'

She hurried away then, back to the ward and her senior's sly questions, none of which she answered. Time enough for Staff Nurse Thomas to hear it from the hospital grapevine.

She was on duty until five o'clock, and just before that time Sister Giles called her into the office.

'You are leaving us, I'm told, Nurse Forbes. A most unusual state of affairs, going off without a moment's notice, but I suppose if Professor ter Laan-Luitinga wishes it there is nothing more to be said. I must say that I am surprised. I hope you will be happy.' She picked up her pen and drew a pile of reports towards her. 'How I am supposed to manage at such short notice, I do not know.'

Venetia murmured sympathetically, guiltily not minding in the least. She was a kind-hearted girl, but she hadn't been particularly happy on the ward, and she saw no reason to pretend otherwise. Indeed, it gave her pleasure to see Staff Nurse Thomas's face when she went back into the ward and told her that she was leaving.

'Ah, I've been wondering when they'd get around to moving you. Where are you going? Geriatrics? About all you're fit for——'

'I'm going to be married.'

'Pull the other one,' said Staff Nurse Thomas, and she laughed unkindly.

'To Professor ter Laan-Luitinga—in a week's time. Goodbye, Staff.'

Venetia whisked herself away before the other girl could say a word.

Her friends were much kinder—eager to hear the details, scenting a romance where there was none, helping her to pack, discussing excitedly what she should wear at the wedding. It was midnight before the last of them had gone to their beds and her things had been stowed away. She was left to lie awake and wonder if she had taken leave of her senses.

She spent a good deal of the next day mooning around the home, washing her hair, doing her nails and deciding what clothes she would need to buy. She had her small nest-egg saved against what Granny had always called a rainy day, but now she went to the bank and drew almost all of it out. The professor's careless remarks about her having nothing fit to wear were very vivid in her mind. She would surprise him. She wasn't sure how, but it was a promise she had made to herself which she intended to keep.

She was ready and waiting by half-past six, with farewells said, her cases by the entrance, and wearing her winter coat again for it was a bitter evening. She greeted the professor quietly, waited while the porter put her cases in the boot, and then got in beside him. Surprisingly, the awkwardness she had been dreading wasn't there. He made a few desultory remarks about the weather, told her the name of the church where they were to be married and the time of the ceremony, mentioned that Lottie was delighted to be going shopping with her, and then relapsed into a restful silence. Venetia, who had been wound up as tightly as a fiddlestring all day, felt herself relaxing. She wasn't sure why, but somehow the professor made everything seem perfectly ordinary and rational.

The Mileses' flat was by the river in one of the new blocks recently built. It wasn't large, but it was nicely furnished and the view from the sitting-room was delightful. Venetia was warmly welcomed, taken to the small guest-room, and then escorted into the sitting-room where the men were sitting by the fire, deep in talk about a patient.

But they stopped as the two girls went in and handed them drinks, and allowed the conversation to become light-hearted. Presently they sat down to dinner, a meal which lasted a long time, since they talked as much as they ate. The professor got up to go later, bidding them a casual goodnight. 'I'll let you know the details in a day or two,' he told Venetia as he went. 'Arthur can pass on any messages.'

Singularly unloverlike—something which Lottie remarked upon as she sat up in bed watching her husband pottering round the room. 'Do you suppose they're in love? I know Duert's awfully reserved, but he was downright casual...and Venetia's such a quiet little thing, he'll swallow her whole.'

Her husband cast her a loving look. 'My darling, I suspect that she'll run rings round him. You see, he's never met anyone like her before. His friends, his women friends, are all charming, well-off and spoilt. Venetia isn't any of these things, although I think that there's probably a good deal of charm hidden away behind that ordinary face of hers.'

'Do you suppose it'll turn out all right?'

'I'll be most surprised if it doesn't. The professor seldom makes a mistake.'

After the routine of the hospital it was pleasant to spend the day shopping with Lottie. Venetia had made up her mind what she intended to buy, and after three days of searching she had a small wardrobe of clothes which she hoped would pass muster under the professor's critical eye. For her wedding she had chosen a wool crêpe jacket and skirt in a deep violet with an ivory silk blouse. She had found a little velvet cap to match, and then spent a good deal more than she had intended on a new topcoat, the same colour as the suit with a wide skirt and a shawl collar. She and Lottie had searched for a long time for shoes and gloves and handbag and, since she needed other clothes as well, they wandered round Marks and Spencer and emerged triumphant with a pleated tweed skirt, several woollies and a couple of blouses.

'You need a pretty dress,' said Lottie.

'Yes, but I must have some new undies and a dressing-gown...'

They found those, too, and, since there was still some money left, spent another day looking for a dress. It turned up on a bargain rail, hunter's-green crêpe, quite plain but, as Lottie pointed out, it would do very well until such time as Venetia could go shopping in Holland.

It was snowing when Venetia woke up on her wedding day. The ceremony was fixed for ten o'clock in the morning, since the professor wanted to return to Holland that same day, and the church was small and old, surrounded by East End streets and expensive new flats in the dock area. Venetia watched Lottie and Arthur leave their flat with Mr Inglis, the orthopaedic surgeon who was to give her away, standing beside her. She felt strange in her new clothes, and dreadfully uncertain; she hadn't seen the professor to speak to for days, and suddenly the urge to turn and run was great, but her companion touched her on her arm. 'Time we went, my dear,' he said. 'You look charming.'

She went down to the waiting car with him. If only Duert would find her charming, too...

CHAPTER FIVE

THE church was dim and rather cold, and smelled of age and damp, but someone had put flowers by the altar steps, and as Venetia paused in the open door Mr Inglis produced a small bunch of flowers from behind it—narcissi, lilies of the valley, pink tulips and violets arranged in a nosegay. They defied the snow outside and the cold stillness of the little church, and she buried her nose in them for a minute. When she looked up she was surprised and delighted to find a number of people in the pews, for she had thought that Duert would have regarded the actual ceremony as something only necessary to his plans, and since she hadn't seen him for the whole of that week she had had no chance to ask.

She began to walk down the aisle with Mr Inglis. The professor was standing with his back to her with Arthur Miles beside him. He looked extremely large and remote, and she wished that he would turn round. She looked away from him and met the smiling faces of several of her friends bunched behind Miss Hawkins, who looked formidable in a no-nonsense felt hat. Even Sister Giles was there, looking bewildered. As well she might, reflected Venetia; she must be the most unlikely bride in the hospital's history.

She caught Caroline's eye and smiled. When the professor did turn round at last, she smiled at him, too, suddenly aware that she would be able to cope with whatever the future held.

The ceremony was simple and brief, and afterwards they all drove to the Ritz Hotel and drank champagne and ate delicious bits and pieces, and presently cut the cake. Venetia, who hadn't expected anything like it, was beaming with pleasure. Standing alone with Duert for a moment, she said, 'Thank you for such a lovely wedding—I never guessed... I thought we would just go to church and get married.'

He didn't tell her that that was what he had intended, and it was Lottie who had organised the whole thing, declaring that Venetia deserved a wedding day to remember. He had agreed unwillingly, and now he was glad that he had allowed Lottie to have her way.

The reception didn't last long; Venetia's case had been taken round to the car before the wedding, so that presently all that she had to do was to wish everyone there goodbye and get into the Bentley beside Duert.

The euphoria engendered by her wedding was still with her, and she chatted happily for several minutes before she realised that Duert wasn't listening. She fell silent then, hoping that he would say something—anything—but he made no effort to speak, and when she peeped at him she could see that his profile was stern. Presently she asked, 'Is anything the matter?'

He turned to look at her then, a quick, impersonal look which chilled her. 'The matter? No, should there be? It all went off very well. Lottie arranged everything very splendidly, I thought.' He glanced at his watch. 'We should be in Leiden by the late afternoon. I'll call in at the hospital and take a look at the man I'll be operating on in the morning—you won't mind waiting in the car? I shouldn't be long, we can drive home afterwards.'

Home, she knew, was somewhere between Leiden and den Haag. Her home now. She had a great deal to think about as they travelled, and plenty of time in which to do so; true, they stopped on their way to Dover for lunch in Wye. The Wife of Bath was a small cottage restaurant, and the food was excellent. The professor, when he chose, had delightful manners. He made sure that she had everything that she wanted, and carried on a casual conversation which never once touched on themselves. Venetia, bursting with questions about her future, and so far given only the barest facts, longed to ask endless questions, but somehow she found it impossible to interrupt his mild observations on this and that with her queries. All in good time, she supposed.

On the hovercraft he became at once immersed in a sheaf of papers from his briefcase, although he had made sure that she had something to read as well. But everything was too novel to waste time with a magazine. She found the crossing fascinating and, when they landed, the business of going through Customs just as exciting; having had her new passport conjured up within a few days by the professor gave her a thrill. But she didn't say so—obviously the professor considered the journey as routine as taking a bus from here to there. He gave her back her passport and swept the Bentley out on to the road which would lead them northwards, through Belgium and on into Holland.

They left Calais behind them, bypassed Bruges and Antwerp, and crossed over into Holland from the Breda *autoweg*. The professor drove past Dordrecht and turned on to the motorway to Rotterdam, then circled away to take the road to Gouda, Alphen and finally Leiden. By then the afternoon was well advanced, and Venetia was longing for a cup of tea. Her heart sank as Duert turned into the courtyard of a large hospital and stopped before its entrance. It rose again when he said, 'You must be longing for tea. Come inside and I'll arrange for you to have it while I'm talking to the anaesthetist.'

The hospital, old on the outside, was mostly modern inside. Venetia was ushered into a small room, nicely warm and well lit, and shortly after the professor had left her a porter came in with a tea-tray. But only one cup, she noted. All the same, she took off her coat, poured her tea and started on the little biscuits accompanying the teapot. The tea worked wonders for her state of mind; by the end of the second cup she conceded that Duert had every right to put his patients first, and that his silence during their journey had almost certainly been due to his preoccupation about the patient he was even now examining. And he had told her that they would see very little of each other, although she hadn't expected it to be quite as soon . . .

Tomorrow, in daylight, she would be able to see around her. From what she had glimpsed through the gloom of the afternoon, Holland was exactly as she had expected it to be: flat, covered in snow and chilly. There had been people skating on some of the canals as they had passed, and the old houses in Leiden looked charming in the street-lights. Delft would be even better, she told herself stoutly, and poured another cup of tea.

The professor returned presently, enquiring if she was ready to leave and, after being meticulously introduced to a small group of hospital staff, she went out with him to the car and was driven away, back into the snowy streets. It was quite dark by now, and once they had left the centre of the town there was nothing to see. After a minute or two she asked, 'Is it far to Delft?'

'About fourteen miles. Are you tired, Venetia?'

'Not in the least.' Hungry and rather scared, now the journey was almost over, but not tired. 'Do you drive to and fro to Leiden each day when you're in Holland?'

'When I'm operating there, yes. I go to den Haag and Amsterdam, too, and quite frequently to Brussels, and occasionally to Hamburg.'

He was driving fast on the motorway, and the lights of den Haag were reflected in the night sky. 'I did tell you that I was often away from home.'

'Yes, you did. You—you don't mind that?' She turned her head to peer at him. 'And your home at Hampstead? Do you mind leaving that?'

'Oh, yes, but I know that I shall be going back there frequently. I think that I have no preference, though; my home is here as well as in England. I am happy in either.'

Presently he turned off the motorway and took the main road to Rotterdam; she could see the lights of Delft now, and felt a glow of excitement, but once more he turned the car from the town, into a narrow road with snow-covered fields on either side of it.

'I live just outside the town,' he explained. 'The house can be reached easily from Delft, but this will be quicker as we have no need to go into the town.'

He drove on for a short distance, and presently she saw a high stone wall, and wrought-iron gates flung wide. The professor turned between the stone pillars on either side of the gateway and drove slowly along a short drive lined with trees and thick shrubs, bare now, and laden with frozen snow. There were lights ahead of them, and Venetia strained her eyes to see the house. They were almost there before she could make out its bulk. It was much larger than she had ever imagined, its many windows pouring light on to the sweep before the front door. It was opened before the professor had got out of the car, helped her out, too, and taken her arm to walk her up the shallow steps to where an old man was waiting for them.

'Domus...' The professor shook the old man's hand, said something in Dutch and drew Venetia forward. 'This is Domus, my trusted butler. He served my father before me and is a family friend.'

Venetia shook hands and smiled at the elderly face with the twinkling blue eyes. He looked friendly, and she felt indeed that it augured well for her future. A moment later, as they went through the vestibule into the hall, an elderly woman, tall and thin and sharp-featured, came from the back of the hall. The professor shook her hand, too, and turned to Venetia.

'And this is Truus, Domus's wife. She used to be my mother's maid, but now she is our housekeeper.'

Venetia shook hands again, and wished she had an idea of what was being said. How in heaven's name did Duert expect her to run his house when she couldn't speak a word of his language?

Unerringly he had understood her hesitant murmur. 'Don't worry, my secretary speaks English and she will help you, and, of course, Anneta speaks English, too. You shall have lessons in Dutch as soon as you like. Domus tells me that Anneta is in the drawing-room at the back of the house. Shall we go there first, and then Truus will take you to your room?'

He sounded friendly enough, but she heard the faint impatience in his voice. He was a man who was used to having his own way, even though he disguised the fact with good manners. She said cheerfully, 'I'd like

to meet Anneta first,' and was rewarded by his faint
smile.

The lovely hall was large and square and panelled
in some pale wood. It was thickly carpeted in a very
dark red and lit by wall sconces—delicate affairs with
crystal drops and loops. Difficult and time-consuming
to clean, she reflected, crossing the hall beside the
professor while Domus went ahead to open the big
double doors at the back of the hall. There was a
staircase beside them, of the same light wood and carpeted in red, which curved up to a gallery above the
hall, but she had no chance to examine it closely for
the doors had been opened and, with the professor's
hand propelling her forwards, she went into the
drawing-room.

It was a large room, and the first thing that struck
her was its comfort. It was grand, too, but there were
comfortable chairs, magnificent curtains at the tall
windows, and plenty of reading-lamps on the small
tables scattered around. There was a great fire, too,
leaping up the wide chimney with its enormous stone
hood.

The girl and the dog sitting by the fire both turned
as they went in, and Venetia felt the professor's hand
on her arm as he spoke.

'Anneta...'

Venetia looked up into his face, and he looked down
at her with a smile of such kindness that her mis-
givings gave way to common sense; she was his wife
and quite able, with his help, to cope with the future.
She watched the girl, who had bounced to her feet
and was coming across the parquet floor towards
them, the dog yelping with delight ahead of her.

Anneta was pretty with fair hair cut short,
enormous blue eyes and a lovely mouth. She looked

older than her seventeen years, due to the clothes she was wearing: a swirling skirt, ankle length, in some soft material; a scarlet silk shirt; and an outsize cardigan, its vivid blue matching her soft leather boots.

'Darling Duert!' she flung herself at him, talking all the while in Dutch while the dog pushed himself between them.

The professor gave a crack of laughter and spoke in English. 'What a welcome.' He disentangled himself and tucked a hand under Venetia's arm. 'Nice to see you again, Anneta. I've a pleasant surprise for you. This is Venetia, my wife.'

'Hello, Anneta,' said Venetia and put out a hand.

Anneta took it slowly, staring at her. 'Your wife? Duert, you never told me you were going to get married.' She smiled suddenly, seizing the hand she was offered, and kissed Venetia's cheek. 'How absolutely super!' She darted a look at the professor. 'Now you'll never have to worry about me again, will you?' she asked airily.

'That remains to be seen,' said the professor drily.

Anneta chuckled. 'Venetia—may I call you Venetia? Duert has had to put up with me for years, but not for much longer now. I think we shall be friends, don't you? I've only had governesses and companions— even when I was at a boarding-school they were waiting for me in the holidays.' She wrinkled her charming nose. 'They always wore brown or black and had absolutely no idea about clothes.' She gave Venetia an appraising look. 'You look smashing. Do say you like clothes, too...'

'Oh, I do,' said Venetia, glad to get a word in edgeways at last, and conscious that Duert was amused. 'I dare say we shall go shopping together.'

'Having settled that important problem, will you take Venetia upstairs? Truus will have got her room ready—I phoned her about it.'

He gave Venetia a little pat on her shoulder. 'You must be famished—I know I am. Will fifteen minutes or so be long enough for you to take off your hat?'

He went with them to the door, opened it, and stood watching them crossing the hall and going up the staircase, before going to his study to glance through the pile of letters waiting for him, the dog with him.

The staircase opened on to a square gallery with several doors and wide corridors leading away on either side. Anneta opened a door at the front of the gallery and ushered Venetia into the room beyond. 'The master bedroom—isn't that what they call it in England?' She crossed to a door and opened that, too. 'Bathroom. There's a door on the other side— Duert's room. He's always used a room at the back of the house, but, of course, now he's moved in here. I never guessed, and I saw Truus moving his things over this afternoon.' She turned a mischievous face to Venetia. 'I can't wait to see the faces of certain ladies I know who have been hoping for I don't know how long to become Mevrouw ter Laan-Luitinga.'

She skipped to the door. 'I'd better go and find Duert and give a faithful account of where I've been and what I've been doing for the last ten days or so. He takes his guardianship seriously, you know.'

Venetia, left alone, took off her outdoor things and then explored the room. It was large with long, narrow windows hung with thick silk curtains, their peach pink echoed in the bedspread and the bedside lights. There were lights on either side of the applewood table with its triple mirror, and someone had set a bowl of blue hyacinths upon it. The carpet was a very pale blue-grey, and soft to her feet, and there was a vast cupboard along one wall. Perfection indeed, and the perfection was echoed in the bathroom, cream-tiled and with its shelves piled high with pastel-tinted towels, little bowls of soaps, bath essences, and just about everything a girl could wish for. She did her face, brushed her hair into tidiness, and went back downstairs rather slowly, shy of going into the drawing-room. The professor must have heard her, for he came out of his study as she reached the bottom stair and crossed the hall to meet her. 'A drink before we have dinner? You like your room?'

'It's delightful, and I'd love a drink.' She paused as they reached the drawing-room door. 'It's all much larger—much larger than I had expected...'

'I think that you will find that it shrinks in size as you get used to it. Remember that it was built a couple of hundred years ago, when it was usual to have large families. Besides, the Dutch at that period liked to build solid houses with their East Indies fortunes. Tomorrow Anneta will take you over the place.' He opened the door and the dog, a black Labrador, lumbered happily to meet them. 'This is Digby, by the way. He belongs to me, but since I'm so often away from home he shares himself among all of us.'

Venetia bent to stroke the dog. 'He must be glad to have you home for a little while.'

'Just as I am glad to be here.'

He fetched their drinks and sat down beside her on one of the vast couches on either side of the fire. 'Anneta will be down in a moment. I shall be away until tomorrow evening, Venetia. I'm sure she will tell you anything you want to know and show you round. The country is pretty around the house, and the garden is a good size. When the weather is settled you can explore. I'll open a bank account for you tomorrow, and you can go shopping in den Haag. You will need clothes, and Anneta will love to help you buy them.'

She said, 'Yes, Duert,' so meekly that he turned his head to look at her.

'You are probably thinking that it is no one's business but your own as to what you should buy. I'm sure your taste is excellent—that is a charming outfit you have on—but, seeing that we shall go out a good deal and entertain here, too, I should like you to have all the clothes you require.' He added in a voice that she had heard often at St Jude's, polite, chilly and quite certain that whatever he wanted would be done, 'And let us be quite clear upon the matter, Venetia— I am quite able to foot the bills, however extravagant they may be, so you have no need to examine the price tags too closely.'

'Oh—well, I'll try and remember not to. Have you a great deal of money?' She went a bright pink and bit her lip. 'I'm sorry, I shouldn't have asked.'

'Why not? You are my wife, you have a right to know. And yes, I do have a good deal of money; a large part of it is inherited, the rest I earn. But be assured that there is ample. If you should need more money than there is in your account you have only to tell me.' He smiled a little. 'I can trust you to be as extravagant as you wish, but I hope you will curb Anneta's wilder spending. She has always had everything she needed or, for that matter, wanted, and it's time she learnt the value of things. She will marry one day and need to be less reckless. Besides, her aunt in America will expect her to have at least a modicum of good sense.'

He got up as he spoke and Anneta came into the room. 'Ah, the two love-birds!' she exclaimed. 'I stayed away as long as I could, but I do want a drink...' She grinned at Duert and went and sat beside Venetia. 'What is it you say in English? I will be a gooseberry.'

'Gooseberries,' said Venetia in her down-to-earth way, 'are hairy and green! I don't think that you are either.'

A remark which delighted Anneta. 'You have no idea how nice it will be to have a friend. Duert, how clever of you to marry Venetia.'

'Rather should we not say how kind of her to marry me?' His voice was as bland as the face he turned towards her.

The three of them dined presently in a panelled room on the other side of the hall, which was hung with heavily framed portraits. They sat at a large oval table set with lace table-mats, heavy silver and crystal. And the food was delicious, served by Domus aided by a stout young girl with rosy cheeks. Venetia, tucking into *poulet à l'estragon*, reflected that it would be easy to adapt to such a pleasant way of life. She looked up and found Duert's dark eyes upon her. She smiled at him, and then blushed because his half-smile and raised eyebrows warned her that he had read her thoughts. But if she felt awkward it was easy enough to conceal with Anneta's chatter, a never-ending stream of gossip about her friends, her clothes and what she would do when she went to America. Duert listened to her courteously, but Venetia had the feeling that his mind was on other things. She thought that he was fond of his ward, but that he found her a distraction. That, presumably, was where she would be expected to do her part—keep Anneta amused and out of mischief so that he could get on with his work. His work meant a great deal to him. If it hadn't been for Anneta and the problem of seeing that she conformed to a conventional way of life, he would never have married. Well, he has married now, thought Venetia, spooning a mouth-watering ice-cream pudding, but all the same he has arranged things exactly to suit himself.

An unkind thought, she conceded, listening with half an ear to Anneta's prattle, for he would be a good husband if one counted material things as vital to a happy marriage. Later, perhaps, when they had got to know each other really well, things might change...

They went back to the drawing-room presently, to sit talking over their coffee, until suddenly Anneta got up. 'Well, I'm for bed—we had rather a lot of late nights at the van Hoeves', and I only got back this morning.' She kissed Duert and then Venetia. 'See you at breakfast.'

If Venetia had hoped that Duert would continue the conversation they had had before dinner, she was to be disappointed. He told her a little about the house and the country around it, made a few observations about Delft, recommended that she should take Anneta's advice as to the shops she should visit in den Haag, and remarked upon the wintry weather. Any minute now he would suggest that she was tired and might like to go to bed...

She agreed about the weather, at the same time getting to her feet. 'I think I should like to go to bed,' she told him without fuss. 'Shall I see you before you go in the morning?'

He had risen with her, and they went to the door. 'I doubt it. I shall leave here at about seven o'clock, and hope to get back in time for dinner in the evening.'

He stood looking down at her, his brows drawn together. 'You have everything that you need? You're comfortable in your room?'

'Oh, it's delightful, thank you. I shall sleep like a top. Goodnight, Duert.'

In her warm, comfortable bed an hour later, she lay going over the day's happenings. It seemed incredible that in that short time she had married, travelled to another country and become someone quite different: Mervrouw ter Laan-Luitinga. She twisted the golden ring on her finger just to make sure about that. And it had turned out to be much less traumatic than she had expected. Anneta appeared to like her, and that was a bonus, for a start. And that had been the main reason for Duert marrying her. She allowed her thoughts to turn to the delights of shopping for suitable clothes. Duert had said that she might have *carte blanche* and she began to make a mental list of what she might need.

She fell asleep in the middle of it.

Duert had been gone for an hour or more by the time she got down to breakfast, but Anneta joined her at the table. 'Truus is dying to take you around the house. I'll come too, if you like, to translate.'

Venetia accepted gratefully and took no offence when Anneta said, 'Is it going to be very different? Living here?'

'Well, yes—very. I lived in the hospital, and my granny, when she was alive, had a small house in Hampstead, where I went on my days off.'

'Did you work with Duert?'

'Gracious, no. I was a second-year student nurse— he's a highly respected consultant surgeon.'

Anneta rested her chin on her hands and planted her elbows on the table. 'I always knew he'd fall in love—properly, I mean—and now he has and you're rather nice. Not pretty, but you do have such lovely eyes.'

'Thanks. What do you mean "properly?"'

'You must know that he's very eligible—is that the right word? He could have married a dozen times since I came to live here, and that's eight years ago. I think you're just right for him.'

Venetia thanked her and wondered what her companion would say if she knew the truth. Luckily she would never know. She asked, 'When do you go to America?'

'In September, it's my birthday on the third, and I'll go to my aunt very soon after that. My father wanted that, and I expect I'll like America.' She shrugged. 'It's quiet here, Duert is away so much.' She smiled suddenly. 'But it won't be any more, of course, now you're here. When shall we go shopping?'

She glanced at Venetia's tweed skirt and sweater. 'Did you bring a lot of clothes with you?'

'Come upstairs and see,' invited Venetia.

'But there's nothing—absolutely nothing!' exclaimed Anneta, having seen Venetia's wardrobe. 'We might go shopping just as soon as we can—today...'

'I'd like to see the house first. I believe Truus is waiting to take us round.'

Anneta pouted. 'She can wait until we're ready. It's more important to get you some clothes.'

'No, it's not.' Venetia made her voice firm. 'Truus has her work to do, and we have all the time in the world. Let's go and get her.'

The tour of the house took a long time—not only was it a large place, but Truus wanted to give each room, each piece of furniture, each picture full attention, and Venetia enjoyed every moment of it. Ig-

noring Anneta's rather sulky presence, she wandered
from room to room, examining cabinets, commodes,
and tables and peering at family portraits.

'What very large families,' she murmured, studying
a painted group of a Regency gentleman who looked
astonishingly like Duert, his hand on the shoulder of
an especially splendidly dressed lady, surrounded by
an artistically arranged bunch of children. 'Eight of
them,' said Venetia, counting.

'Duert likes children,' whispered Anneta and
giggled. 'You've got a busy time ahead of you,
Venetia.' She stared at Venetia. 'You're really quite
pretty when you blush.'

When they had visited the entire house they went
into the gardens. The snow had stopped falling and
everything was quite white and still. In thick coats
and scarves and boots chosen from a selection in the
lobby beyond the kitchen, they went outside.

'If we have lunch early we could go to den Haag
this afternoon,' suggested Anneta. 'We can't start too
soon on your clothes.'

Venetia agreed. 'If you'd tell Truus?' She would
have to learn to speak Dutch, basic Dutch at least, as
quickly as possible. She registered a resolution to ask
Duert to arrange lessons as soon as he could; she was
at a disadvantage until she could at least order the
meals and understand Truus and Domus.

A youngish man, who saw to the gardens and
greenhouse and drove the car when necessary, took
them into den Haag. There were two cars there beside
the Bentley Duert drove—a Jaguar and a Mini. They
went in the Jaguar, and Venetia made another vow to
learn to drive, so that she could use the Mini without
depending on anyone else. Anneta had had lessons,
but she had been forbidden to drive. 'Duert says I'm

not careful enough—just you wait until I get to America.'

She knew just where to go once they reached den Haag. 'Not my usual shops,' she explained, hurrying Venetia through arcades and narrow streets. 'You're not quite my style, are you? More the doctor's wife—oh, do you see what I mean? I know the very shop to start with.'

The shop, when they reached it, didn't look very promising to Venetia, who had been used to High Street stores where she could rummage round the rails, checking the prices and looking for bargains. There was one garment in the window, a silky dress flung carelessly over a little gilt chair. A pale scarf had been tossed on the carpeted floor beside it. 'I don't think that's me,' said Venetia doubtfully.

But once inside she was swept into an inner room and shown one outfit after another. 'For the day,' explained Anneta, 'you'll need at least three dresses...'

Quite carried away, Venetia tried them all on, finally choosing a slim skirt with a matching top in a pleasing shade of blue, a wool dress in dove grey belted in soft leather, and, gently egged on by Anneta, a wide jersey skirt with a matching top in navy blue with a cropped cardigan, embroidered all over with pale pink roses, to match. And not once did she look at a price ticket. In any case, it seemed likely that such an elegant shop wouldn't have any such thing. Everything was charged to Duert and they left the shop, very pleased with themselves.

'A cup of tea,' declared Anneta, 'and then another boutique that's just right for you.'

'But I've already bought three outfits.'

'But you can't wear them in the evening.' Anneta dragged her into a small, elegant tea-room, ordered tea and produced a list. 'I dare say you have a list, too, but this one will be better. I dare say you've crossed out a list of things you think you don't need.'

Venetia nodded guiltily. 'Well, yes—it's such a long list.'

'You don't have to worry about saving Duert's money,' said Anneta gently. 'He's—what do you say?—loaded.'

'Oh, well, then perhaps one more dress—something pretty for the evening...'

The boutique was close by and even more elegant than the first shop had been. Venetia came out of it half an hour later with a triumphant Anneta beside her. They were loaded with dress boxes, and Venetia felt slightly light-headed. She now possessed three more dresses, all, so the sales lady had assured her in almost perfect English, suitable for a quiet evening at home. A plum-coloured velvet with a sweeping skirt and long, tight sleeves, a patterned crêpe de Chine, skilfully cut with a pleated skirt, and a misty grey crêpe patterned with pastel flowers. There was no doubting the fact that each of them did a great deal for her, she had hardly recognised herself in the salon looking-glass. True to her promise, she hadn't asked the prices; she only hoped that Duert had meant what he had said.

Apparently he had, for, beyond admiring the plum velvet that evening and expressing the hope that she had bought a few things for herself, he showed no anxiety over the bills. He had returned home in time for dinner, and joined them in the drawing-room, looking as though he had never done a hand's turn in his life, although Venetia thought that he looked tired. But he joined in the general talk with every appearance of enjoyment, and only after they had dined and had their coffee did he excuse himself with the plea that he had some dictating to do.

'He dictates into that machine,' explained Anneta, 'and Juffrouw Floos types it all out each morning, but perhaps now he's got you he will spend more time here in the drawing-room. You don't get much time together, not during the day...'

Venetia agreed gravely. She must remember that she was there to present a picture of solid married life. 'I dare say it will take Duert a few days to catch up with his cases in Leiden. He's such a very busy man.'

'I'm a bit scared of him,' confessed Anneta suddenly. 'I'm never quite sure what he is thinking.'

Venetia agreed heartily, but silently. She said bracingly, 'You don't need to be. I think he would be upset if he knew that.'

'You won't tell him?'

'Of course not. I hope we'll be friends, and friends don't tell tales on each other.'

'Promise you'll never tell tales on me, Venetia...'

'I promise, because I don't think I'll ever have cause to do so.'

'You are nice. I'm so glad Duert found you. Tomorrow we'll go to the kitchen and you can order the meals—I'll help you—and then we'll go to den Haag again. You need a coat and boots and undies and a couple of evening dresses for a start...'

They fell to discussing the latest fashions in winter coats until Duert came back and Anneta went to bed, and since he didn't seem disposed to talk to her Venetia went to bed, too. She wished him a friendly good-night, assured him that she had had a delightful day, and whisked herself away. He had been pleasant and beautifully mannered, but she felt shut out.

So what did you expect? she asked herself, going upstairs and listening to the door closing behind her.

CHAPTER SIX

IT WAS astonishing to Venetia to find how quickly she settled into her new life. The house ran on oiled wheels and, although she saw Truus each day about the meals, arranged the flowers and went through the contents of the linen cupboards, she had nothing much to do. Yet her days were filled. Anneta was determined to turn her into what she called a fashionable young wife, and, although some of her ideas were rather more than Venetia could accept, she knew which shops to go to, and within a week Venetia had acquired a wardrobe carefully planned to cover any social occasion, as well as more mundane tweed suits and woollies.

Venetia found herself wondering why Duert had been so anxious to have someone in his home to be with Anneta. The girl seemed contented and happy enough, even though her clothes were sometimes outrageous and she was at times silent. She seldom spoke of her school and the friends she had made there, and the young people who came to the house seemed harmless enough, even if noisy. Venetia met them all and, being not much older than they were, enjoyed herself with them. She would have liked to have told Duert this, but she only saw him for short stretches of time each day, and Anneta was almost always there.

When they did find themselves alone he had little to say, other than polite enquiries as to whether she was settling down, had enough money, was ready to start Dutch lessons...

To all of which she replied in her sensible way that everything was fine and the lessons couldn't be started soon enough as far as she was concerned.

It was at the beginning of the second week that Anneta told her that she had an appointment with the dentist. 'I go to a man in den Haag. He's good, but very slow. I arranged to go while you have your lesson in the morning, then we can go out in the afternoon if you like.'

'How will you go?'

'I'll get a lift in the car—the gardener's going in for some bulbs, and if I'm not ready he can come on home and I'll get a taxi. It's only a mile or two.'

Venetia, her lesson over, was in the garden, crunching through the frozen snow, muttering Dutch verbs, when she heard the car coming back and went off round to the garage to meet Anneta. She wasn't there. Wim, the gardener, shook his head and smiled and then said, 'OK, *mevrouw*,' with which she had to be content. It was almost lunchtime when she heard Anneta's voice as she came into the house, and she hurried out to meet her.

'I was getting quite worried,' she began. 'Are you all right? Was it very painful?'

Anneta flung a careless arm around her shoulders. 'Not too bad, but I went and had coffee afterwards and sat for a bit. I hate the dentist.'

They went together into the dining-room. 'Well, at least it's over for six months,' said Venetia.

'Oh, no. I have to go again in a week's time, but I'd like to forget that. What shall we do this afternoon?'

'If you don't mind, I'd like to take a look round Delft. Would that bore you?'

'Dear Venetia, of course not. We will tour the churches, and then have tea and be home in time for Duert.'

So the afternoon was spent pleasantly enough, and when Duert came home there was so much to talk about, Venetia quite forgot about the visit to the dentist.

Anneta was spending the evening with friends, so Duert and Venetia dined alone, sitting with the width of the table between them, carrying on the kind of conversation which might have been made by polite acquaintances. Finally, Venetia, tired of remarks about Dutch architecture and the weather, asked, 'Which hospital were you at today? And did you operate? Have you a long waiting list?'

The professor looked surprised, and then said, 'Forgive me, I'm not used to anyone asking me questions about my work.'

'Well, you don't have to talk about it if you don't want to,' said Venetia matter-of-factly, 'but I'm interested.'

'I do believe you are. I have been in den Haag operating on a man who fell from a scaffolding—rather a lengthy business, but I hope that he'll be all right eventually. And yes, I have a short waiting list, although you must realise that most of my surgery is of the urgent sort.' He stirred Digby gently with his foot. 'Do you have enough to do, Venetia? You are not bored?'

'Good heavens, no. Now I've started my Dutch lessons they take up quite a lot of the mornings. Besides, Anneta and I go out quite a lot, you know, and her friends come here for coffee and tea.'

'You like them?'

'Yes—of course, I don't know them well, but they're all very pleasant, even though I don't know what they're talking about half the time.'

'I should like her to do something useful with her time.'

He frowned in thought and she said quickly, 'She's only seventeen, Duert. Couldn't she just enjoy herself until she goes to America?'

'Do I seem harsh to you? I have no wish to be, but the headmistress of her school became uneasy about her. She went off on her own from the school on several occasions, and she is careless of convention. I'm not sure that all of her friends are good for her.'

'And what do you want me to do?'

'I think that you are doing all that you can. She likes you and she listens to you and enjoys your company, which is more than could be said for her governesses and companions.'

A compliment—even if a tepid one. 'Thank you,' said Venetia, and earned a quick, frowning look.

He said testily, 'My work takes me from home a good deal. I have had to rely upon various ladies...'

'Well,' said Venetia soothingly, 'now you don't need to any more. I'm here, aren't I?'

She picked up the tapestry work she had begun; she wasn't very good at it, but she guessed that she would have plenty of time in which to improve. She stole a good look at him and saw that he was staring at her. A habit he had got into which she found a little disturbing. She said thoughtfully, 'I have been wondering if it might be a good idea if I did some kind of work...' She watched his eyebrows fly up and went on hastily, 'By that I mean some kind of charity—there must be children's homes or geriatric wards where I might help once or twice a week, and I think

I might persuade Anneta to come with me. She has no idea of how the other half lives, you know.'

'That's a very good idea. I'll see what there is in Leiden, and there's a children's hospital in Amsterdam. You don't mind what you do?'

She shook her head. 'Anything to help out. There's another thing, Duert—I'd love to learn to drive a car.'

'Why not? Would you like Wim to teach you in the Mini?'

'Yes, please. Anneta can drive, she tells me.'

'But she's too young. She is also a bad driver. Have you ever driven?'

'No.' She wondered if he remembered what a restricted life she had lived before he married her, and thought it unlikely.

He picked up the sheaf of papers on his knee. 'I must go and deal with these. By the way, we may expect invitations very shortly from friends and colleagues. Drinks and dinner and the usual hospital balls.'

'How nice,' said Venetia faintly. What a blessing that Anneta was there to suggest what she should wear.

At the door he said, 'Anneta should be back shortly, say goodnight to her from me, will you?'

She watched his vast form go through the door. He shut it gently behind him, leaving her alone with her tapestry.

Anneta came home presently, sat for a moment to talk about clothes for the dinner parties, and then, declaring she was tired, went to bed. She had looked rather flushed, Venetia thought, but that was probably due to the warmth of the room after the cold night outside. She sat on for some time, but Duert didn't come back, so she went to bed, too.

The first of the invitations arrived the next morning, and Duert, breakfasting with them for once, handed it to Venetia. *'The Burgermeester,'* he observed. 'Drinks and dinner. Black tie and long dresses. Get a dress and anything else you want. Anneta, you are invited, too.'

'I don't want to go, thank you. A lot of dull, middle-aged fuddy-duddies telling me what a big girl I've become.' She pouted prettily. 'I need not accept, Duert, darling?'

'You will accept, and come with Venetia and me. It is time that you learn a little about the polite world, or you will be at a great disadvantage when you marry.'

'Venetia doesn't know anything about the polite world, and she manages quite well.'

Venetia made a business of buttering toast, and hoped that no one would notice her blush.

'You will apologise for that remark,' said Duert, 'and I can hope only that when you eventually marry you will behave with the same charm and grace as Venetia.'

Venetia thought he was laying it on a bit thick, but it was nice of him, all the same. She received Anneta's apology with a smile and a murmur that she knew she hadn't meant it anyway. 'And it would be lovely if you came with us. Duert won't be with me all the time, and I shall feel quite lost.'

Anneta's expression was sulky, and the professor's face wore the bland look which she was fast becoming aware covered impatience. 'We might go to den Haag,' said Venetia rather hurriedly. 'I don't think I've got anything quite grand enough.'

Anneta brightened at the prospect, and Duert picked up the letter he had begun to read, and the meal was finished with everyone on good terms with everyone else.

Invitations came thick and fast. Some included Anneta, but not all, and Venetia, ably tutored by her, answered them all in her neat writing, worried away at her Dutch conversation, and spent a good deal of money on clothes. To Anneta's suggestion that she might go to a fashionable hairdresser and have her hair arranged more elaborately she said a firm no, although she did agree to wear rather more make-up. She dressed for the *Burgermeester's* dinner party in some trepidation. Her dress was new and deceptively simple with its full skirt and long-sleeved bodice with its low-cut neck; its russet-brown silk flattered her mousy hair and gave her grey eyes a sparkle, and she tripped downstairs, her cheeks pink with excitement. She had dressed early and there was no one about. She crossed the hall, admiring her bronze slippers as she went, and entered the drawing-room. Digby came to meet her, and she patted his head as she went to the hearth to examine her image in the vast mirror to one side of it. She gazed critically at her person, rotating slowly, her head over one shoulder, trying to get a back view.

'Very nice,' said the professor from one of the big wing-chairs by the window. 'You have no need to worry, Venetia. You look charming from every angle.' He got up and came to where she was standing, and she saw that he was already dressed. 'I'm glad you came down early; there is something I want to give you.'

He had a long velvet case in his hand and he opened it now to reveal a double row of pearls. He took them out and said, 'Stand still while I put them on. They were my mother's, and my father's mother's before her, and *her* mother's before that.'

She had turned obediently so that he could fasten the jewelled clasp. 'Oh, but I can't possibly wear them...'

He said evenly, 'You are my wife, Venetia, and they are in your keeping now.' He turned her round to face him. 'There is something else—a little late in the day, only something I overlooked before we married.'

He put a hand in his pocket, took out a small box, and lifted the lid. There was a ring inside—a sapphire surrounded by diamonds in an old-fashioned setting. 'My mother's,' said the professor, and he slipped it on to her finger above her wedding ring.

She looked up at him uncertainly. It had seemed to her quite logical that a marriage such as theirs hardly merited any outward show of an affection which didn't exist. 'There is no need——' she began.

'No, but I wish it, Venetia.' He smiled, and bent and kissed her—not the usual peck on one cheek which he was careful to give her when, as so often, Anneta was there, but a kiss to stir her to a pleasurable warmth. It was pure ill fortune that Anneta should come into the room just at that moment, to stop short when she saw them and exclaim, 'I'm interrupting! Shall I go away and come in again?'

The professor released Venetia without haste. 'Why should you do that? It is normal practice for man and wife to kiss upon occasion.'

Anneta looked at Venetia's pink cheeks. 'Actually,' she said slowly, 'it must be rather nice. I mean, there's kissing and kissing, isn't there?'

'As you will discover for yourself one day.' He had kept an arm around Venetia. 'If you are quite ready, we should go.'

Anneta twirled in front of him. 'Well, do I suit your ideas as to how a girl should dress? Venetia persuaded me . . .'

He studied his ward and nodded his head. 'You look delightful, and very correctly dressed, too.' He smiled down at Venetia. 'How did you do it?'

'Anneta has excellent taste. I didn't have much say in the matter.'

Anneta dropped a careless kiss on her cheek. 'You really are a nice person, Venetia. I can quite see why Duert wanted to marry you.'

Venetia busied herself checking her little evening-bag, and didn't look up. She wondered what Anneta would say if she knew the truth.

The *Burgermeester's* gathering was a splendid affair. He stood at the head of the great staircase in his house, his wife beside him, and greeted his guests. He was a tall, stout man with a magnificent beard and moustache, and his wife was almost as tall and certainly as stout. They greeted Duert as an old friend, kissed Anneta and shook hands with Venetia, beaming at her.

'So nice,' said the *Burgermeester's* wife, 'that Duert is now married. We shall hope to see much of you, and there are many here tonight who wish to meet you.'

Venetia wasn't aware that she was a success; she had never attracted much attention at St Jude's, or among her friends in London, and she hadn't expected it here, only hoped that she would pass muster. But she was liked at once—not only because she was Duert's wife, but because her quiet charm and ability to listen were a refreshing change from the usual party gossip. She went in to dinner with a colleague of Duert's, Dr van Tiele, who teased her gently about

her smattering of Dutch, expressed his hope that now
Duert was married he would cut down on his work,
and asked her about her life in England. She talked
to her other partner, an elderly man whose English
was heavily accented and who talked endlessly about
fishing, and she turned with relief to Dr van Tiele
again.

'And Anneta? You get on well with her? You are,
perhaps, a good influence on her. I haven't seen her
so sensibly dressed for a long time—so well behaved,
too. She has given Duert a good deal of trouble, but
I expect you know that.'

'We get on very well; happily, she has been a great
help to me. Perhaps she was bored. I've asked Duert
to see if there's any kind of work we could do at one
of the hospitals. Not nursing, just helping around once
or twice a week.'

'My dear lady, if you can persuade Anneta to
employ her time usefully you will indeed have wrought
a miracle.'

She didn't see him again to talk to, for after dinner
the ladies sat together for a time gossiping until the
men joined them, and presently everyone went home,
leisurely departures involving a good deal of chatting
on the way to their cars.

Back home Anneta said at once, 'I'm dying for my
bed. What a boring evening. I'm so glad I haven't
been invited to that dreary drinks party with the
Gieringers.' She kissed Venetia, pecked the professor's cheek, and ran up the staircase.

Venetia made to follow her, but Duert caught her
by the hand. 'No, stay for a little, Venetia. Truus will
have left coffee on the stove.'

He urged her through the door at the back of the
hall and into the kitchen, warm and redolent of coffee

and the after-taste of a well-cooked meal. He stared
down at her and then sat her by the Aga, and Digby
and Truus's cat both opened sleepy eyes, yawned and
closed them again.

The professor strolled round his kitchen, gathering
mugs, coffee, sugar and cream with the air of a man
who had done it many times before. When he had
assembled everything to his satisfaction he poured the
coffee, offered Venetia a mug and went to sit opposite
her by the Aga.

'This is very pleasant,' he observed. 'Usually I
return from one of these evenings and go straight to
my study or to bed, but now you are here to mull over
the party with me. Did you enjoy yourself?'

'Very much, thank you. I shall enjoy it even more
when I can understand Dutch and speak it a little.'

'It seemed to me that you were managing very well.
Van Tiele was enchanted by you, and so was the
Burgermeester who, I must tell you, is very much a
ladies' man.'

It would have been nice, thought Venetia, sipping
her coffee, if Duert had found her enchanting, too...
She said quietly, 'I'm glad they approved of me.
Anneta looked very pretty, didn't she? She's a very
lovely girl.'

'Her mother was a beautiful woman—an American.
It was tragic that she should have died so young and
that her father should have been killed in a car crash.
I have done my best, but I sometimes think that I
could have done better. I must admit that you have
already done a great deal to steady her down.'

Venetia could think of nothing to say to this. She
finished her coffee, put her mug tidily in the sink and
declared her intention of going to bed. The professor
was looking forbidding and she didn't know why. She

wished him goodnight and rustled her way upstairs, wanting very much to be on more friendly terms with him. Just for a moment that evening, when he had given her the ring, she had thought that perhaps their relationship was developing into something warmer, but now she doubted it.

He had gone when she went down to breakfast the next morning, and Anneta was still asleep. The post had arrived and the professor had opened it and left a small pile of invitations by her plate with a scrawled, 'We had better accept all of these,' written across the top envelope. Which sent Venetia into a worried reverie about clothes once more.

It was surprising how quickly the weeks passed. They went out a great deal, and sometimes she wondered if that was entirely to Duert's liking. To come home after a long day in the theatre and Out Patients and have to change and go out again, with almost no time to do more than snatch a hurried cup of coffee and a sandwich, seemed to her to be burning the candle at both ends with a vengeance. Not that he appeared tired. All the same, she ventured to protest one evening as they drove to yet another dinner party.

She had short shrift. 'It is expected that you should be introduced to my friends, and now that we are married they wish to meet you. Besides, it helps to keep Anneta amused.' He drew up before an old town house in Delft where they were to dine. 'I think it is almost time for us to give a dinner party ourselves. Several.'

Anneta had accompanied them to almost all the drinks and dinner parties to which they had been invited. She had been compliant, but Venetia had a feeling that the girl's willingness to go along with her guardian's wishes wasn't as whole-hearted as it seemed. What was more, Venetia was beginning to wonder about the dental appointments which, considering the perfection of Anneta's teeth, seemed excessive.

'What exactly is wrong with your teeth?' she asked one morning in as casual a voice as she could muster.

Anneta had launched into a lengthy description of fillings and dental surgery which Venetia found hard to believe, and one morning, after another rather dull dinner party, when the girl had come downstairs with the news that she had yet another appointment with the dentist, she had voiced her uncertainty, to come face to face with a very different Anneta.

'You may be Duert's wife, but you have no right to pry!' she stormed. 'Is that why he married you? To spy on me? You're no better than those awful companions...'

'Why should I need to spy on you?' asked Venetia calmly. 'I merely wanted to know about your teeth.'

Anneta was instantly full of apologies. 'Darling Venetia, I didn't mean to be so snappy. It must be all these late nights. And anyway, this will be my last appointment.' She glanced sideways at Venetia. 'Did Duert want to know when the dentist would be finished?'

'Not that I know of. I've not mentioned it to him.'

It was disquieting to see the look of satisfied relief on Anneta's face.

By now Venetia had her life organised. Her Dutch was coming along nicely; her conversation was limited, but she could understand Truus well enough, and even shop without nearly so much difficulty. She hesitated to speak Dutch to Duert or Anneta and, since they spoke English with the same fluency as they spoke their own language, there seemed no need to do so.

All the same, she found that she was beginning to understand the language, sometimes to her disquiet.

Anneta had invited some of her friends for coffee one morning in late February. The snow had long since gone, and now and again there was a fine day, still cold, but with a hint of spring in the air. On such a morning they had all spilled out into the gardens, Venetia with them. She had walked a little apart, not wanting to intrude into their laughing chatter, but after a time she realised that she was understanding what they were saying among themselves. Anneta's voice, carelessly loud, was easily recognisable even in Dutch, although Venetia missed some of the words.

'My dears, she knows nothing. I have been going to the dentist—' there was a spate of laughter at that '—for weeks now, and she believes me. She is very nice, but she is also trusting. I have no difficulty with her. So tomorrow you, Hilde, will telephone and ask me over for lunch.' They all laughed and she went on. 'You, Piet, will be waiting with the car as usual. Where shall we go?'

Venetia missed the rest of it, but she had heard enough. And what was she supposed to do about it? Only one thing seemed adequate.

She decided, and said loudly, 'Just a minute. I don't speak much Dutch, but I can understand it, and I've heard everything you've just said—enough, at any rate.'

She faced half a dozen surprised young faces. 'Anneta is in my care, and until she goes to America she should do as her guardian wishes. So forget this outing tomorrow. Hilde—which of you is Hilde? Please don't telephone, and Piet...' She glanced round her. 'There will be no outing.'

Anneta turned on her. 'I suppose you will tell Duert?'

'Why should I do that? Don't be silly, Anneta, his work keeps him busy enough and worries him enough without your pranks. Now let's go indoors and have some more coffee.'

Thinking it over later, she wished that she and Duert had a closer relationship. He was kind and considerate and treated her with an impeccable politeness which chilled her, but he wanted no contact with her, and evinced no desire to talk to her; only from time to time he would ask about Anneta very much in the same way as he might ask a ward sister how his patients did. Perhaps when we get to know each other better, she mused, we could talk—really talk—and not just make conversation.

With help from Duert she and Anneta went twice a week to help at the children's hospital in Amsterdam. She wasn't sure if Anneta liked going very much, but *she* certainly did. The children were sweet, and since they had only the convalescents to feed and amuse for the afternoon their work was not onerous. Wim drove them, and just once or twice they had gone with Duert when he had had occasion to consult with one of the surgeons there. And on these occasions Venetia had sat in the back of the car; it seemed to her that Anneta didn't see enough of her guardian and, indeed, it did improve matters, for the two of them laughed and joked together in their own language and she, watching them, was aware of satisfaction. It was not quite perfect, though, for she was conscious of a feeling of loneliness, too, but that was dispelled when they reached the hospital and Duert took her arm for a moment.

'I'll be here waiting for you,' he told her, and smiled kindly down at her, just as though he knew what she had been thinking. She had answered him briskly—pity was the last thing she wanted from him, and she thought that she had seen that in his smile.

Spring came reluctantly, but when it did it made up for its tardiness with a succession of sunny days, still cold, but not so cold that daffodils didn't bloom in their hundreds around the house. The formal beds were filled with early tulips and crocuses, and Wim had a boy to help him, and sometimes when the professor was free he dug and planted and weeded. Venetia didn't ask if she might help; she got into her Marks and Spencer skirts and sweaters and marched outside to give a hand, and Duert, beyond a look of surprise, said nothing. Indeed, she had the impression that he was pleased to have her there. Anneta stayed indoors. She hated gardening, she explained, and she always had a good excuse—a book to finish, a letter to her aunt in America, her wardrobe to turn out . . . Venetia, planting out hyacinths under her husband's critical eye, tried to make up her mind about the girl. She was almost always friendly—affectionate even—willing to join in anything Venetia suggested, and just lately discarding the strange garments she had always worn. And yet there was something not right, and Venetia couldn't put her finger on it.

It was on a Sunday afternoon, while gardening happily beside Duert, that she scratched her wrist above the gardening glove with a thorn on a dead twig. Duert pulled off the glove and looked at it. 'You'd better go in and clean it,' he suggested. 'It's only a scratch, but you can't be too careful. It's not painful?'

'My goodness, no—if you hadn't been here, I'd have sucked it and gone on weeding.'

He laughed. 'Well, I am here, so off you go!'

She had gone into the house, smiling to herself. It seemed to her that just now and again she caught a glimpse of Duert—the real Duert. The house was quiet—Domus and Truus would be in their sitting-room behind the kitchen, and the maids would be at home for the afternoon in Delft. She went through the back door and into the hall, taking off her wellingtons as she went, mindful of the polished floors, and had a foot on the bottom tread of the staircase when she heard Anneta's voice. She was speaking from the small sitting-room behind the dining-room and her voice sounded clearly. She was telephoning, and Venetia pottered across the hall and pushed open the half-open door.

'Hello,' she said. 'Is that anyone for Duert?'

She was quite unprepared for Anneta's reaction. She whirled round, blazing with rage.

She raged, 'How dare you? Sneaking up on me like that—how long have you been there, listening? Did Duert send you in to spy on me?' She looked at Venetia's stockinged feet. 'Creeping round the house...'

Venetia made her voice matter-of-fact. 'Well, I can't tramp around in a pair of muddy wellies. Why are you so cross? I heard your voice as I came in, and came to see if it was a call for Duert.' She watched Anneta put the receiver back. 'And don't let's have any nonsense about spying. This is your home, and no one has ever questioned your using the phone if you want to.'

She turned away, but Anneta ran across the room and caught her arm. 'Darling Venetia, don't be cross. I'm so sorry I snapped, but you startled me. I was only chatting to Mieke—you know, the girl who was at school with me.'

'I'm not cross.' Venetia smiled at the pretty face, which was not scowling any more. 'I'm on my way to clean a scratch. I'd better do that, or Duert will want to know why I haven't.'

'You won't tell Duert?' She could hear the sudden panic in the girl's voice.

'No, of course not.'

'Promise?'

'I promise.' She went upstairs to wash her wrist, puzzling about Anneta. She was up to something, some small escapade quite likely, but Venetia wondered why she had been so furiously angry.

Back in the garden, Duert paused in his digging. 'Just lately,' he observed, 'you have looked worried. There's something wrong, isn't there? You're happy here? Our—er—our arrangement is perhaps not ideal, but I think that we are very much benefiting from it— both of us. You are certainly fulfilling your side of the bargain.' And when she protested that she was happy and content, 'Then there is something else, or should I say someone else? Anneta? You have changed her remarkably. If you had known her before...but perhaps you can't talk about it.'

He waited, and after a moment she shook her head, not looking at him.

'I thought as much. All right, I won't ask you, but I think I can help. Leave it to me!'

He didn't say any more, only began a discussion as to what would look best in the bed he was digging. They were debating the choice of massed stocks when Anneta, huddled into a coat, came out to join them.

She stood between them and caught them each by the arm. 'You know, when I see you two together I could almost believe that being married must be quite fun. Perhaps I'll decide to settle down, after all.'

'What were you intending to do?' asked the professor casually.

'Oh, have fun until I'm thirty or so. One is past it at thirty.'

He agreed gravely. 'Probably you will meet some young millionaire while you are living with your aunt.'

'Must he be a millionaire?' asked Venetia.

Anneta squeezed her arm and giggled. 'Of course he must. Don't forget that I'm used to living with one.'

Venetia just stopped herself in time from looking at Duert. She had known that he was well off, but she had never thought of him as rich. She said lightly, 'It does make life easier, and there must be dozens of millionaires in the USA.'

They all went indoors then, and had tea round the log fire, and just for once the professor spent the whole evening in their company. It wasn't until she was in bed that Venetia, going over their talk, came to the conclusion that he had asked a great many cleverly designed questions of Anneta. He had said that he would help, but she couldn't think how. Besides, he was so deeply immersed in his work.

But he hadn't forgotten; several days later they were at breakfast when he opened a letter, read it and observed carelessly, 'This seems to be more for you than me, Anneta,' and passed it across the table to her.

She read it slowly, and began smiling. 'I say, Duert—this sounds like fun. I haven't seen Lucille for ages.' Her smile faded. 'But I suppose you won't let me go.' She passed the letter to Venetia and turned to her guardian.

'I don't see why not. You've grown up a lot in the last month or so, and it will be a splendid chance to see something of Paris.' He looked across at Venetia. 'What do you think, my dear?'

The letter was from the Netherlands Embassy in Paris, from someone who signed herself Marijke, and it suggested that since her daughter was celebrating her eighteenth birthday in ten days' time they had hit on the idea of inviting her schoolfriends to stay for a week, so that they could all celebrate the event. 'I shall take good care of her,' went on the writer, 'and we shall be delighted to welcome her.'

'What a marvellous idea,' said Venetia. 'Was she a friend of yours, Anneta?'

'Lucille? Oh, yes, we were in the same class. Duert, please may I go?'

'Yes, of course. Marijke is an old firm friend of mine, and so is her husband. You must write and accept, and we will arrange the journey.'

'I'll need heaps of clothes.'

'We'll arrange those, too, but nothing, I beg of you, too ultra.'

Anneta danced round the table to hug him. 'You really are an old dear!' she cried. 'We'll go to den Haag today and start buying.'

'And I'll go to den Haag and do a day's work.' He got up from the table, kissed them both and drove himself away, leaving them to plan a wardrobe.

He got back late that evening, listened patiently to Anneta's description of the clothes she had bought, told her that he would see about her flight the next day, and took himself off to his study after dinner. It was much later, when Anneta had been in her room for an hour or more and Venetia was sitting in the drawing-room with her tapestry, that he joined her, Digby at his heels.

He sat down opposite her. 'You are a most pleasant companion,' he said, to her surprise.

'But I haven't said a word.'

'That is what I meant. Do you suppose this trip to Paris will solve your problem for you?'

'Oh,' she lifted her lovely eyes to search his face. 'I did wonder... Yes, I'm sure it will. You must know a great many people.'

'Yes, I do. Venetia, I'm going to take a week off. I have an aunt living at Salcombe, I think that we might pay her a visit. Would you like that?'

'Salcombe? That's south Devon, almost Cornwall. Oh, yes, I would.'

'Good. No need to tell Anneta, and you won't need a vast new wardrobe.'

Her mind was already on sandy beaches and woods and sea. She turned a beaming face to his. 'That's the last thing I'm thinking of!'

CHAPTER SEVEN

ANNETA'S journey was arranged for a week ahead, and the days between were taken up with the shopping she found essential for her trip. Venetia went with her to den Haag almost each day, going patiently from one boutique to the next while Anneta gathered together a wardrobe far in excess of what she would need. And when she remonstrated all Anneta did was to shrug her shoulders and declare, 'Well, Duert can afford it, and why shouldn't I have all the nice things I want?'

'But think of the excess baggage on the flight,' ventured Venetia.

'I always have excess baggage,' Anneta told her. 'I shall buy some clothes in Paris, of course.'

'In that case, I see no need for all these outfits you've bought!' said Venetia tartly. 'You're just wasting Duert's money.'

Anneta tossed her head. 'Sometimes, Venetia, you are quite miserly. That gold tissue dress we saw today, and which would have suited you very well—you would not buy it...'

'I didn't want it,' Venetia pointed out. 'I've all the dresses I could possibly need and, besides, me and gold tissue don't go together.'

Anneta considered this. 'Perhaps you are right. You are what I think is called a *jolie laide*, and you cannot be ultra smart.'

Venetia accepted that opinion in good part. 'Yes, well, never mind about me—what about that corduroy suit we saw today? It would be just right for travelling.'

They saw little of Duert. He had gone to Brussels for a consultation and stayed away for two days, and it wasn't until very late at night that Venetia heard the Bentley stop before the door. In the morning, although she had got up early, he had already gone again.

Not satisfactory, she decided; he was obsessed by his work, as though he were trying to escape from an ordinary life. He had always seemed to be detached at St Jude's, and if she had thought of him at all it had been with awe, and certainly no curiosity as to his private life. But now she knew more of that, and although she still stood in awe it was more of his work than of him as a person. She began to wonder how they would get on at Salcombe.

They drove Anneta to Schiphol after lunch at the end of the week, and waited there until they saw the plane airborne.

'We'll have tea in Amsterdam,' declared the professor. 'I'll have to go to Leiden in the morning, but I thought we might leave directly after lunch tomorrow. We'll stay the night in Hampstead and drive down to Salcombe the next day. My aunt lives alone with a housekeeper and an assortment of dogs and cats. She is mildly eccentric—my mother's elder sister, widowed. Her house is on the opposite bank of the estuary, facing Salcombe, and the grounds go down to the beach.'

He was driving towards Amsterdam, not hurrying.

'We shan't need to dress up?'

'No. I dare say we'll dine out, but you'll not need a long dress.' He sped past an articulated lorry and then slowed again. 'How are your driving lessons going?'

'Wim says I'm doing well . . .'

'You can understand him?'

She answered him in passable Dutch. 'Of course, and I speak Dutch to him. We understand each other very well.'

'My dear Venetia, what a delightful surprise, and how hard you must have worked. I had no idea . . .'

'Well, of course you hadn't.' She spoke tartly. 'You never asked, and why should you? It's not all that important.'

'There you are mistaken,' he said blandly. 'It is most important, and I have been blind not to have seen it.'

She sat and worried over that remark until they were in the heart of the city. He took her to the Amstel Hotel and gave her tea in a solidly comfortable room overlooking the river, and then drove her back home. She went indoors filled with the pleasure of a delightful afternoon, and the hope that at last he was beginning to regard her as a friend. Her hopes were dashed within minutes, for as he came into the hall behind her he told her casually that he would be at the hospital at Leiden until late that evening. 'A meeting I must attend,' he told her, apparently without regret. 'I'll see you at breakfast.'

So she had a solitary dinner and went early to bed, filling in the empty hours with packing a case with sensible clothes suitable for Salcombe. The elegant outfits she had been wearing were pushed to the back of her wardrobe. Instead, she folded the Marks and Spencer skirts and woollies, and added one pretty dress just in case they were to go out one evening, and then, on second thoughts, folded a black satin skirt and a chiffon blouse as well. Stout shoes and a woolly cap completed her rather sketchy wardrobe, as well as her oiled cloth jacket in case the weather turned nasty. She gave a good deal of thought to what she would travel in. They would be staying the night at the Hampstead house, so she packed another small overnight-bag with a taupe jersey dress and an extra blouse, and decided on a tweed suit and a thin cashmere jumper. No hat—she would be in the car for most of the time, and a Gucci scarf Anneta had given her would cover her head if it turned cold or wet.

More or less content with her choice, she went to bed, to lie awake until she heard Duert come quietly up the staircase and go to his room.

Beyond reminding her to be ready to leave when he arrived home, Duert had little to say at breakfast.

'You won't be home to lunch?'

'I'll get a sandwich before I leave the hospital. Anneta should phone some time during the morning.'

'Shall I tell her we're going to your aunt's?'

He smiled slowly. 'No—tell her we will ring her, she need not ring us. We will keep our holiday secret, shall we?'

'Very well.' Venetia buttered toast and took a bite.

She found that his smile disorganised her common sense. It was still more disorganised when he added, 'I have thought lately that I should like to get to know you, Venetia.'

She swallowed the toast, lost her breath and had to be thumped gently on the back. When she had her breath back again she said quite inadequately, 'Yes, well—if you want to. There's nothing much to know...' Her voice trailed away under his amused stare.

He got to his feet, ready to leave. 'As to that, you must allow me to be the judge.' He came round the table and bent and kissed her cheek—not the usual peck for Anneta's benefit, but leisurely and gently. Left to herself, she poured more coffee, offered Digby a piece of buttered toast, and reflected that she knew even less about Duert than he did of her.

She was waiting for him when he got back very shortly after lunch, her case in the hall, she herself sitting without fidgeting in the sitting-room in her expensive tweed suit and the cashmere jersey. He paused to look at her as he came in, remembering that months ago he had told himself that she would repay dressing, and she did; she looked very attractive, pretty even, with her hair curling softly round her face. She had nice hands and feet, well gloved and shod, and her handbag was exactly right. He wasn't a very observant man when it came to women's clothes, but he had to admit that she looked good. He said 'Hello. How nice you look.' Which surprised her so much that she pinkened and blinked her eyes.

The pink made her pretty, he came a little closer. 'Did I ever tell you how restful you are?' he asked.

'No. Have you had a busy morning?'

'Very, but everything I needed to do is done. Will you mind coming over to Hampstead for a few weeks when Anneta gets back? I've several cases at St Jude's. A change of scene might be good for her.'

And what about me? thought Venetia silently. Would it be good for me, too, or don't I come into your plans? 'That would be nice,' she said sedately.

The Bentley took them swiftly south to Boulogne and, once across the channel, up the A20 and the M20 to London. They were in Hampstead in the early evening, with Todd and Mrs Todd waiting to welcome them and offer them congratulations once more.

Venetia was borne off to a magnificent bedroom at the front of the house, where a beaming Mrs Todd opened cupboards and drawers and showed her the bathroom. 'And the professor's room is just through the other door.' She twinkled. 'His dressing-room, I should say.'

Venetia had a shower and got into the jersey dress, which, after all, was a waste of time for Duert, emerging from his study, told her that he would have to drive over to St Jude's and get his dates fixed. 'Don't wait dinner,' he told her, 'but I should be back quite early.'

Rather obstinately, she asked Mrs Todd to hold dinner for an hour, so that when he did get back, some time after eight o'clock, it was there waiting for him.

'You've not dined?'

'No. Mrs Todd has got such a splendid meal for us, I thought I would wait a while...'

'That was thoughtful of you.' He spoke pleasantly, but evinced no pleasure at the idea of her company, although he carried on an easygoing conversation as they ate. But as soon as she had poured their coffee he excused himself once more with the plea of paperwork, wished her goodnight and went away to his study, leaving her puzzled. He had seemed pleased at the idea of their holiday—even hinted at getting to know her better—but she had to admit that he showed no urge to substantiate either.

And yet, at the back of her mind the idea was forming that he was changing his opinion of her. 'It must be the clothes,' she told the empty room, and went to bed.

They set off directly after breakfast the following day under grey skies which threatened rain, but it was, after all, April now, and the weather could change from hour to hour. Which it did before they were half-way to Salcombe. They stopped for coffee just before Honiton, and then drove on until they reached Buckfastleigh and took the road to Totnes. There was a nice old pub just off the road and Duert slowed the car.

'This looks all right for lunch.' He turned to look at her. 'And it's not raining. You're not tired?'

'Not a bit.' She skipped out of the car with the sudden feeling that they were at last on holiday, and, now she came to think of it, they hadn't been out together since she had stayed with Lottie.

They had no need to hurry over their meal. Salcombe wasn't all that far now, and the Bentley ate up the miles effortlessly and at speed. They drove through Totnes and on to Kingsbridge, and finally along the narrow road alongside the estuary.

Salcombe came into view on the far bank, a small town straggling along the water's edge, its cottages and villas interspersed with a few hotels, huddled cosily together, the town church on the hill above them, and yachts anchored in and around its small harbour.

'There's a ferry,' explained Duert, 'otherwise it means driving up to Kingsbridge and then back on the other side. My aunt's house is at the end of this lane.'

They were passing substantial houses, some old, some not so old, their backs to the lane, their gardens running down to the wide, smooth sands beyond, but presently they gave way to a rocky coastline, still with wide stretches of sand. The sea was ahead now, not far off, the tide coming in with a flurry of waves, tossing the lobster boats on their way to the harbour. And at the end of the lane, where it petered out to a track leading down between the rocks to the sands below, Duert stopped. There was a double garage built into the stone wall beside the lane, and a small gate beside it. He opened it and ushered her through on to a path which led to a porch and an inner door.

As they reached it it was flung open and a small round body bounced out. 'There you are!' she declared. 'And the tea just this minute made.'

She beamed at the professor, who drew Venetia forward. 'How nice to see you again, Meg. Venetia, this is Meg who looks after Aunt Millicent.'

Venetia shook hands and was studied by a pair of very shrewd blue eyes. 'Well, now,' said Meg comfortably, 'isn't that nice? Come on in, your aunt's in the drawing-room.'

The house faced the estuary, its garden falling down to a fence protecting it from the rocks and the beach beyond. The room they were shown into at the back of the house had a magnificent view of Salcombe on the further side of the estuary as well as a wide view of the open sea. There was an enclosed patio beyond the room, and someone was sitting there. Aunt Millicent. Venetia had tried to imagine her from the sparse facts Duert had supplied, but the reality wasn't anything like her imaginings. Aunt Millicent was Miss Marple in the flesh, small and grey-haired, dressed at least thirty years behind current fashion, and presenting a mild, almost self-effacing appearance with a presence which Venetia found totally disarming.

She came to meet them as they went in. 'How delightful, my dears. Duert, it is a long time since you have visited me, and now you have brought me your

wife.' She bent forward to kiss Venetia. 'I am so delighted to meet you, dear.' She smiled gently at
Venetia, who smiled back rather shyly. 'And so exactly right for Duert. His father was a marvellous
man, you know, but he needed managing, and his
mother did that very well, just as I'm sure you will.'

Venetia murmured and avoided Duert's eye, sus-
pecting that he was secretly amused.

'Meg shall take you up to your room, and then we
will have tea. I like to sit here at this time of the day—
such a lovely view.' She called to Meg, who was hov-
ering in the doorway. 'Meg, take Mevrouw ter Laan-
Luitinga up to her room, will you? And we'll have
tea in ten minutes.'

The room Venetia was led to overlooked the estuary, its windows opening on to a wide balcony; it
was well furnished with rather heavy Victorian furniture, and the walls were papered with a large rose
pattern. The bathroom beyond was old-fashioned,
too, but had everything one could wish for, and when
Meg opened a door in the far wall there was a smaller
room, rather severe. 'Mister Duert's dressing-room,
ma'am. Mrs Reynolds thought you might like to have
these rooms because of the view.'

'They're lovely,' declared Venetia, 'and so
comfortable.' She went back to the bedroom and
peered at her reflection in the massive looking-glass.
She didn't look too bad; she powdered her nose and
used some lipstick and, since Meg had gone downstairs, spent five minutes exploring the room. She was
going to be happy here, she could feel it in her bones.

Downstairs she found her hostess and Duert
standing at the open french windows, watching the
lobster boats chugging towards the harbour. The

afternoon had cleared and a watery blue sky had turned the sea to a dim blue, too.

'A good day tomorrow,' said Duert, turning to look at her as she joined them. 'We will be able to walk over the headland, if you would like that, or perhaps you would rather go over to Salcombe and explore the town?'

Venetia had joined them at the window. 'Well, if it's going to be a nice day a walk would be heavenly. We can always go to Salcombe if it rains.'

Meg brought in the tea and they sat over it, the conversation undemanding and then presently, from Venetia's point of view, interesting, as Aunt Millicent began to reminisce about her youth, Duert's mother and father, and Duert's boyhood.

'I saw a good deal of you in those days,' said Aunt Millicent, 'and we came over to Holland frequently. I haven't been for years...'

'Would you visit us?' asked Venetia, and looked at Duert in case she had said the wrong thing. But she hadn't; he looked very pleased.

'Why not?' he joined in. 'I'll come for you in the car and bring you back.'

'That would be delightful. But I should prefer to come after Anneta has gone to her aunt. A dear child, but so lively!'

'Then that's settled—some time after the beginning of September.'

Aunt Millicent nodded gently. 'Yes, dears. Now go for a stroll; it is such a perfect evening now, and we don't dine until eight o'clock.'

'I'll fetch the bags in first.'

Duert went away and Aunt Millicent said, 'Such a dear man, my dear. I'm sure you must be very happy.'

'Yes,' said Venetia, 'I am,' and found to her surprise that it wasn't a polite social lie, but the truth. And when Duert came back she said, 'I'd better change my shoes.' She went upstairs again and got out her sensible low-heeled lace-ups, still feeling happy. When she had the time to think she would find out why, in the meantime she mustn't keep Duert waiting.

He glanced down at her shoes as they went through the gate into the lane. 'Ah, good—I shan't need to lift you over the rocks.' He spoke casually and she took instant umbrage, although she was careful to murmur a nothing in reply. Why, she pondered, had he bothered to bring her with him if that was how he felt about her?

They started down the wide track at the end of the lane and he broke a silence stiff with her hidden resentment. 'I did put that badly, didn't I? Rest assured that I am willing at any time to carry you any distance necessary—or unnecessary, for that matter.'

He tucked an arm in hers. 'I'm feeling very much in a holiday mood. I hope you are, too?'

"Well, yes, I am.' Everything was all right again, and she looked up at him and smiled widely. 'It's absolutely heaven here, isn't it?'

His dark eyes stared down at her grey ones very thoughtfully. 'I do believe that you are right.'

They had reached the sandy beach and cove at the bottom of the track, and they crossed the sand to stand at the water's edge. Although it was a clear evening, lights were already showing on the opposite bank and the little town looked cheerful.

Venetia took a deep breath. 'Oh, doesn't it smell gorgeous? All salty and clean. I feel quite different...'

'And so do I,' said Duert and, very much to her surprise, kissed her. He took his time about it, too, and then stood with his arm around her, saying nothing, and indeed she was content for it to be so; for the life of her she could think of no suitable remark to make.

Presently he said, 'We had better go back. Aunt Millicent is a stickler for punctuality.' He spoke in his usual rather cool manner, and Venetia, still devoid of a conversational gambit, nodded without speaking.

If the professor had been feeling different on the shore, he showed no sign of being so that evening. She went down to dinner in the pretty dress to find her hostess and Duert in the drawing-room, and, although he got up and fetched her a drink, he had become his usual detached self—politely so, but detached, nevertheless. She went to bed after a pleasant evening, feeling vaguely unhappy about it, although the last thing she thought about before she went to sleep was the way he had kissed her. She smiled at the memory as she dropped off.

They set off after breakfast the next morning, and, since it was a blustery day and rain threatened, she was wearing one of her skirts, with a sweater, and on top her oiled cotton jacket. Her head she left bare, and instead of the elegant french pleat she had become accustomed to she let her hair fall on to her shoulders. The wind would toss it around whatever she did with it, and she thought it unlikely that Duert would notice. She was sure that whenever he had complimented her on her appearance it had been for Anneta's benefit and not hers, and the occasions had always been when she had been dressed up to go to an evening party or dinner.

They went down the track again and across the cove, and took the narrow path winding through the trees which came down almost to the water's edge. They followed it, still close to the water, to Gara Rock and on to Prawle Point, where they stayed for a while, the wind buffeting them and the sea foaming on the rocks below.

Venetia lifted her face to the rather wintry sun. 'Oh, this is heaven.' She closed her eyes and then opened them again to look at Duert, leaning against a rock close by. He looked different, she decided; perhaps it was the clothes he was wearing, trousers and a sweater over an open-necked shirt. He was very good-looking—even when he was in one of his testy moods he was a handsome man, and he had no conceit...

He turned to look at her, not smiling, not indifferent either, just thoughtful. She stared back at him, hoping that nothing of her sudden surge of feeling showed in her face. To fall in love with him had never entered her head, but she had, with a suddenness which was, to say the least, inconvenient. And not so sudden, she reflected, he had never been far from her thoughts for weeks now.

He was frowning now. 'What is going on behind that quiet face, Venetia?' he wanted to know.

That would be the very last thing she told him. So far they had managed very well; a model married life when Anneta was around or when they went out, but never a hint of anything more. Indeed, when they had been alone he had invariably excused himself on the plea of work to be done. And the kiss yesterday? Well—there hadn't been anyone else about, had there?

'Nothing,' she told him airily. 'Just a nice muddle of thoughts—this sea air has gone to my head.'

'Yes? And only the first day.' He smiled a little. 'You're not too tired to go back through East Prawle? We can get coffee there—there's a pub.'

'I'm not a bit tired, but coffee would be lovely.' She smiled, too, intent on behaving as she always did, friendly and undemanding.

What was she going to do? she wondered, following his broad back along the narrow path. Unthinkable to tell him, and there were still more than four months to go before Anneta left for good. Carry on, she supposed, and when Anneta had gone, she could tackle the problem.

She jumped guiltily when Duert said, 'I've said the same thing twice, Venetia, and you haven't heard a word.' He stopped suddenly so that she cannoned into him and needed an arm to keep her on her feet.

'So sorry,' she said, very conscious of the arm and wishing it would stay forever. 'I was thinking,' she cudgelled her brains for a suitable subject to think about. 'Anneta,' she said, in such a relieved voice that he frowned again. 'You know—wondering how she's getting on. She's such an attractive girl. She'll love America, don't you think? I do hope...'

She peeped at him. He was smiling, but not nicely. 'Oh, dear, what have I said to make you smile that way?'

'Like what?'

'Well, you smile like that when you lecture the nurses and one of them makes a silly reply to a question.' She paused. 'Ready to pounce.'

He roared with laughter. 'Am I such an ogre? Do you think I am an ogre, Venetia?'

It would be best not to tell him what she thought of him. 'No,' she told him sedately. 'I've never thought that, you've always been kind to me.' She added, suddenly bold, 'When you've remembered that I'm here.'

He said blandly, 'Oh, but I've never forgotten that.' A remark which left her puzzled, and hunting for a suitable reply.

They had coffee at East Prowle, and presently went on their way. Inland now, but high enough to get a splendid view of the sea and the estuary. The path was wider now, so they walked side by side, carrying on a desultory conversation which never once verged on the personal. And in between their spurts of talk Venetia brooded on how much she loved him. A difficult man to love, she reflected and, suddenly assailed by a desire to know more about him, asked, 'Have you ever been in love, Duert?'

He turned a bland face to her. 'Well, well! And what has that to do with the lobster boats we were discussing? Yes, of course I have—a dozen times.'

'But you didn't marry any of them?'

His voice was silky and rather cold. 'Only you, Venetia.'

'Yes, but I'm different, aren't I?'

'Most decidedly.'

She said in an uncertain way, 'And do you suppose you'll ever fall in love again?'

'Why do you ask?'

'Well, it would complicate things, wouldn't it?'

'Most decidedly. But I fancy I have settled my future...'

'Oh, you've met someone you love?'

'You are most remarkably persistent. Yes, I think you might say that.'

'But you can't do anything about that until Anneta goes to America?'

'That is correct.' He sounded unconcerned, and she walked on, making rather absent-minded replies to his gentle flow of talk. Anneta would be going in September—the very beginning of the month—and it was already April, only four months away, so what chance had she against this unknown girl who had stolen his heart? She sighed. None at all.

They were back in good time for lunch. Venetia went away to tidy herself and get into a thinner sweater, and when she got down to the drawing-room Aunt Millicent and Duert were discussing the right time of year in which to prune the roses. He got up to get her a drink and eased her into the conversation. His manners were faultless, even though, at times, glacial.

Aunt Millicent retired for a nap after lunch, and Duert, with a word of apology, went into the small library to telephone. Which left Venetia by herself. It was still blustery, with little spurts of rain, but Venetia felt that to sit still and think was an impossibility. She got her jacket again, put on her sensible shoes once more and let herself out of the house.

The tide was coming in, although there were still yards of beach. She wandered through the garden, through the little gate and down the path to the sands, and started walking towards the open sea, across the cove, and on to the rocks beyond. The path they had taken that morning was higher up, and she supposed that it could be easily reached from the rocks. She would go back that way. It was fun scrambling over the slippery rocks, but tiring, too. She was almost at the mouth of the estuary when she realised that the tide had come in much more rapidly than she had expected. She stopped and looked behind her, and saw that the rocks she had clambered over were already veiled in spray from the waves the wind was whipping up. She looked around and decided that she would have to go on for a bit until the rocks were easier to climb. She went on slowly now, stepping carefully from one slippery rock to the next, looking for an easier place to climb to the path above. Only there didn't seem to be one, and the tide was rising...

She stood still, and when, from a long way off, she heard Duert's bellow, 'Stay where you are and don't move!' she did that, not sure if she were more frightened of his cold annoyance or the advancing sea.

He was coming down from the path, going lightly from rock to rock, making nonsense of his sixteen stones. He fetched up beside her, breathing rather fast, his frown so fierce that she braced herself against it.

'The tide comes in very fast,' he said pleasantly. 'I should have warned you. Do you think you can manage to climb up to the path if I give you a hand?'

She stared at him and he stood patiently, faintly smiling. At last she said, 'I thought you'd be furious with me...' she heaved a sigh '...you looked quite ferocious.' When she saw his smile widen she smiled, too, and added, 'Yes, of course I can climb up there—well, I think I can.'

He took her hand. 'Keep at my heels, and don't leave go of my hand. It's slippery and steep.'

She glanced ahead of her. It looked impassable, too, but if Duert could come down with the aplomb of a man descending an easy staircase then she would have to do her best to go up it in the same way.

It wasn't easy. Despite Duert's large, firm hand she slipped and slithered, muttering and mumbling in a voice squeaky with fright, but he didn't pause, holding her firmly in a comforting clasp, and after what seemed an age they were back on the path. She stood panting with his arms around her, her head pressed against his great chest, listening to his steady heart-beats. She could have stayed like that forever, but that really wouldn't do. She pulled away and he let her go. She said, in a voice stiff with her efforts to get back to their normal manner towards each other, 'Thank you very much, Duert. It was silly of me to go off like that . . .'

'Why did you?' He put out a hand and tucked her wildly blowing hair behind an ear. 'Did you want to be alone?'

'No. No, of course not. I thought you were going to be busy and that you wouldn't want to be disturbed.'

His rather stern mouth twitched with a faint smile. 'Sometimes it is pleasant to be disturbed.' He looked up at the sky. 'It's going to rain—do you mind?'

'Not in the least.'

He kissed her cheek gently and took her hand. 'In that case, we'll go back for tea.'

Aunt Millicent was waiting for them in her comfortable, rather old-fashioned drawing-room, looking more like Miss Marple than ever.

'A pleasant walk, my dears?' she wanted to know. 'It is so lovely here, and the walks are a delight—especially for the young and active.'

She poured tea from a very beautiful Georgian silver teapot into paper-thin cups patterned in roses. 'What plans have you for tomorrow?'

'We would like to take you out to dinner, Aunt,' Duert said easily. 'I'll take the car and drive round to Salcombe—we might go to the Marine Quay.'

'Oh, delightful, dear boy. I shall look forward to that. Does Venetia know Salcombe at all?'

'Not yet. I think we might go over by the ferry tomorrow and spend a few hours. We'll stay out for lunch, if that fits in with your plans...'

'Perfectly.' She smiled across at Venetia. 'You will like our little town, my dear, and there are one or two very good dress shops—you may see something you fancy. I'm sure Duert is the most generous of husbands.'

'Oh, yes, he is. I have everything I could possibly want.' Except love, she added silently, but to be fair, there had never been any question of that.

She fell in love with Salcombe. It was a bright morning with a chilly wind as they got into the ferry, and even well within the estuary the water was choppy as the little boat chugged towards the landing-stage. There were steps to climb when they landed—dozens of them—which brought them on to the main street, more or less empty of tourists at that time of the year. 'Coffee?' said Duert, and crossed the road to a small café and urged her inside. Over coffee he suggested what they should do with their day.

'Presents,' he remarked. 'The Todds, Domus and Truus, chocolates for the maids, and Anneta will expect something. And you, Venetia, what would you like?'

'Me? But I have everything, Duert.' Well, almost everything, she thought.

He said casually, 'Oh, well, perhaps we will see something...'

They strolled along. The street was long, running parallel with the water, and it was crammed with shops. Venetia stopped at almost every one, and a surprisingly patient Duert stood while she peered at local pottery, old silver and some rather nice paintings. And when she expressed her liking for some small painted wooden ducks he bought them for her. She thanked him—and meant every word of the thanks. This, she considered, was the first present he had given her that mattered. He had never queried the bills for the clothes she had bought; he had given her his mother's pearls and her ring, but that was because he'd really had no choice.

She clutched the ducks to her and beamed up at him. 'Oh, isn't this fun?' she cried. 'But we should be looking for presents—what can we get for Anneta?'

She discovered an antique silver mirror, its price enough to have kept her and her grandmother in comfort for a month, and added it to the ducks. Then she found local pottery for the Todds, and gossamer-fine handkerchiefs for Truus, and as for Domus, since he smoked a pipe when he was off duty, she suggested a pipe, the choosing of which she prudently left to Duert.

They lunched in a pub by the harbour, off crab sandwiches and, in her case, a glass of white wine, leaving Duert to drink beer. They walked to the end of the little town afterwards, and crossed a footpath which took them in a roundabout way back into the town, and since they stopped frequently to admire the view or watch the yachts going to and fro it was time for tea by the time they found themselves back in the main street. They had said that they would be back for tea, and the ferry was waiting. Content with her day, her cheeks nicely pink, her hair a little wild, Venetia went through Aunt Millicent's gate and paused at the door.

'That was a lovely day,' she told Duert. 'I did enjoy myself, thank you.'

He didn't speak, only nodded as he opened the door for her.

Aunt Millicent was waiting for them, sitting behind the tea-tray, looking a little vague, but pleased to see them. Not that she was in the least vague; Venetia had listened to her talking to Duert, and knew that her mild countenance hid a sharp brain and a probing eye. Not too probing, she hoped.

They dined out that evening, driving up one side of the estuary and down the other to the Marine Quay Hotel, where they ate deliciously and at leisure at a table overlooking the water and the further bank. Indeed, they had an excellent view of Aunt Millicent's house. The restaurant was surprisingly full, but not in the least noisy, and there was no piped music, only a man at the piano, gently playing snatches of this and that.

On the whole, content with her day, Venetia slept dreamlessly.

The days went too fast. They walked in all directions, took the ferry over to Salcombe and idled away the hours, sitting in the sun porch, listening to Aunt Millicent's gentle voice reminiscing about her youth.

On their last morning Venetia got up early and crept through the quiet house and down the track to the cove. It was going to be a bright day and everything was clean and fresh in the morning sun. She took off her tights and shoes and walked barefoot in the sand, dipping cautious toes into the water. It was ice-cold, but delightful. She paddled along towards the outcrop of rocks at the far end of the cove, humming to herself in a breathy little voice, to stop short at the sight of Duert, sitting on a flat rock half-hidden by the trees which grew so close to the sands.

'Oh, good morning.' She skipped away from the water, and curled her cold toes in the sand. 'It's such a glorious day,' she explained.

'Good morning, Venetia. Are you saying goodbye?'

She nodded. She would probably never return to this heavenly spot. She had been careful not to think about the future, but she felt in her bones that, once Anneta had gone, it spelled uncertainty for her.

'I shall have to come over to St Jude's in a couple of months' time—I think that you and Anneta might like to stay in Hampstead. She's bound to want to shop for America!' He turned his dark eyes on her. 'It isn't so long now, and she must make a round of visits before she goes.'

'You will miss her?'

'Heavens, yes.' He spoke coolly. 'She is a dear girl, and she has lived with me for some years, and I have become fond of her. All the same, she has been a problem. I have become self-centred, and my work is all-important to me. I resent anything or anyone interfering with it.'

She said, 'Yes, of course.' After all, that was his reason for marrying her. And since he fell silent she muttered, 'Well, I'll go back. I must dry my feet...'

She hadn't gone more than a few yards when she found him beside her.

'I've got seats for the *Phantom of the Opera* this evening, I thought you might enjoy it.'

She thanked him gravely, her love bubbling up inside her and threatening to boil over at any minute. Probably after today she would see him only at meals when he was at home, and when they were bidden to some dinner party or other. She summoned up a smile; she would have to make the best of it. And not get bogged down in self-pity, either.

CHAPTER EIGHT

THEY left directly after breakfast, and Aunt Millicent bade them a gentle goodbye and added the wish to see them again as soon as it could be arranged. 'Perhaps when Anneta has left you?' she suggested, watching Duert reversing the Bentley out of the garage. She laid a hand on Venetia's arm. 'Things will be easier then, my dear.'

'Easier?'

'You are perfectly matched,' observed Aunt Millicent, 'only he hasn't discovered that yet. No, I am mistaken—he has discovered it, but he is ignoring it. It was unexpected, you see.'

Venetia had gone a bright pink. She said, 'Yes, it was. I—I love him.'

'Yes, dear, I know. But you are sensible and patient. Now run along, and come and see me when Anneta has gone to America.' She patted Venetia's arm. 'Both of you, of course.'

It was a two-hundred-mile drive to London; they left soon after nine o'clock, stopped for coffee and then lunch on the way, and got to the Hampstead house by teatime. Once they were past Buckfastleigh and the narrow country lanes, the roads were wide and the traffic sparse. They could have got there much earlier but they had lingered over lunch. Duert had turned off the A303 at South Petherton and taken her to Le Tire Bouchon, and she had enjoyed the delicious food, her worries for the moment forgotten as they mulled over their days at Salcombe. But although

Duert had told her how much he had enjoyed their stay there, he made no suggestion that they should return. Indeed, within minutes of their return he went away to his study, remarking as he went, 'Perhaps you would ask Mrs Todd to let us have dinner early? And warn her that we shall be back in about two or three months' time—with Anneta of course.'

So Venetia took herself off to the kitchen. 'I'm sorry, Mrs Todd,' she explained. 'The Professor did tell me that we would be going to the theatre this evening; I should have phoned you from Salcombe...'

Mrs Todd regarded her with a motherly eye. 'Don't you worry about that, ma'am. It's a nice fricasseé of chicken, and I can serve it up just as soon as he is ready for it. And if you would let me know a day or two before you come it'd be a help with the shopping. Gentlemen never think about such things, and many's the time the professor has walked in and me with nothing fit to set before him.' She beamed at Venetia. 'But there, they do say that professors are absent-minded, don't they?'

Venetia agreed. The particular one she had in mind could also be impatient, irritable and bent on getting his own way at all times. He was also the nicest man she had ever met. Such a pity she had had to fall in love with him... She was recalled to her surroundings by Mrs Todd wanting to know if she could serve a freshly made treacle tart after the chicken. 'Or if you'll be wanting to get to the theatre, perhaps it had better be something easy—ice-cream?'

'If we had dinner in really good time there would be no reason why we shouldn't have the treacle tart, Mrs Todd. It's one of the professor's favourites, and yours are so delicious.'

Mrs Todd preened herself. 'Well, ma'am, I must say they're well thought of.'

The ladies parted company, and when Todd got back to the kitchen Mrs Todd remarked, 'A real lady, that's what she is, thinking of the professor all the time. No beauty, but that's only skin deep, anyway. I hope that Anneta doesn't give her too hard a time of it.'

'From what I hear they get on like a house on fire.'

It seemed a good opportunity to wear the satin blouse and skirt. Venetia dressed with more than usual care, arranged her hair in its french pleat, did her face nicely and went downstairs to find Duert in the drawing-room. There was just time for a drink before Todd appeared to say that dinner was served, and they crossed the hall to the dining-room, carrying on the kind of conversation Venetia was now adept at. General topics uttered politely, and just as politely answered for the benefit of the household. They were half-way through the treacle tart when Todd came to say that the professor was wanted on the telephone, and, saying that he would take it in his study, he left the table with a word of apology.

He was back again within a few minutes. 'Arthur has phoned,' he told her. 'I told him I would be back here this evening.' He didn't sit down again. 'There's a head case in—he thinks that I might be able to deal with it. I'm sorry that we shall have to miss the theatre—you could go alone...'

'It doesn't matter in the least,' said Venetia, uttering the lie so convincingly that she almost believed it herself. 'I'm quite tired after that long drive, and we have another journey tomorrow.' She even managed to smile at him.

He took the tickets from his wallet and put them on the table. 'Perhaps one of your friends from St Jude's is free?' She could hear the impatience in his voice; he might be standing there within feet of her, but his mind was already with his patient.

He bade her goodnight then, and a few minutes later she heard Todd opening the front door. She finished the treacle tart on her plate, drank the coffee Todd brought, and as she left the table picked up the tickets. 'Todd, the professor told me to do what I liked with these tickets, and I can't bear to waste them. I'd like you and Mrs Todd to use them.' She glanced at the clock. 'If you hurry you'll just get there in time. You've got your car, haven't you?'

Todd looked taken aback. 'The dishes, ma'am, the table to be cleared—Mrs Todd will want to wash up.'

'Just ask her to put everything in the dishwasher, Todd, and I'll clear the table. It will give me something to do.' She added to clinch the matter, 'I'm really quite glad to go to bed early—it's been a long day.'

'Well, if you say so, ma'am.' Todd picked up the tickets. 'I must say Mrs Todd is partial to a good musical, and this one's well spoken of.'

They were on the point of leaving when Mrs Todd ventured, 'The professor, he won't mind, ma'am?'

'He'll be delighted that the tickets haven't been wasted.'

'You'll be alone in the house...'

'The professor won't be late, and I'm not nervous. Have a nice evening.' When they had gone she tidied the dining-room, set the breakfast in the small room beyond the drawing-room and went along to the kitchen. She didn't understand the dishwasher so she left it to its work and, with one of Mrs Todd's pinnies over her pretty clothes, made a good job of the saucepans. Then she put the coffee-pot on the Aga, locked the kitchen door and windows, and went back to the drawing-room. She drew the curtains, although it wasn't quite dark yet, and fastened all the doors and windows, and then, with everything done, sat down with her tapestry work. The house seemed very quiet—usually the two maids were there, but they had been given time off as the master wasn't at home. Venetia went upstairs and spent a long time in the bath, then she washed her hair, did her nails and wandered down to the kitchen to make a warm drink. She was returning through the hall with a mug of cocoa when the front door was opened and Duert came in.

He paused on the threshold when he saw her, his eyebrows raised.

'Surely Mrs Todd . . . ?' he began and then, 'You're not ill?'

'Of course not—I'm never ill,' she added with a touch of defiance. 'I've sent the Todds to the theatre—it seemed such a pity to waste the tickets.'

He put down his case and crossed the hall deliberately until he was within inches of her. 'And you?' he wanted to know in what she privately called his nasty voice. 'You have enjoyed a quiet evening?'

She refused to be intimidated by the edge to his voice. 'Oh, yes, thank you. I washed my hair and all that kind of thing. Did you operate successfully?'

'Yes. Your cocoa is getting cold.'

'Would you like some? Or there's coffee on the stove?'

'Coffee, and I'll get it. Go into the drawing-room. There's the last of the fire there, isn't there?'

He joined her presently, sitting in the big armchair opposite, the mug in his hand, watching her composedly sipping her cocoa, her hair clean and bright from its washing, bare feet thrust into ridiculous pink satin slippers which matched the frivolous dressing-gown she was wearing.

'I seem to have been missing something,' he observed blandly.

'Oh, what?'

'A home life—domesticity, connubial bliss. Why have I never seen you in a dressing-gown in Delft?'

She chose to treat his remark seriously. 'Well, I think Anneta would have found it rather strange. Besides, you are always busy after dinner, working in your study.'

'And you minded?'

'Even if I had, that would have been no reason to change your evening routine. Besides, we went out a good deal in the evenings.'

'So we did—and if my memory serves me we seldom had the opportunity to exchange more than half a dozen words.'

She kept her eyes on her cocoa. 'No—well...' She gave him a level look from her lovely eyes. 'That's what you wanted, wasn't it?'

'Yes, that was what I wanted, Venetia.' He spoke quietly and lapsed into silence. Presently he said, 'I'm sorry about this evening, we will get tickets for the same show and go when we come over with Anneta.'

'That would be nice,' she observed and thought, but not the same as just the two of us on our own. She got up. 'I'll go to bed. I expect you want to make an early start in the morning.'

'Yes, I must look in at Leiden when we get back, but I must go to St Jude's first thing. Arthur wanted to know when they were going to see you again; they want you to see the baby.'

She paused on her way to the door. She had sent a present when the little boy had been born, but beyond a letter or two she was rather out of touch with Lottie. 'Oh, I'd love to see him—perhaps when we come over?'

He had the door open for her. 'Goodnight, Duert. It was a lovely holiday, thank you.'

She went to bed and wept herself to sleep for, although she loved him so much, she had no idea how to break down the barrier of reserve he had built up against her.

They were away by ten o'clock, and back in Leiden that afternoon. Duert had offered to drive her to Delft and then return to the hospital, but she sensed that he was impatient to stop in Leiden. 'It's still quite early,' she pointed out in her matter-of-fact way. 'I'm quite comfortable in the car, why not call in on your way home?'

She saw that he was relieved at that, but when they got to the hospital he took her in with him, saw her into the consultants' room and arranged for her to have a tea-tray. 'I don't suppose I shall be too long,' he told her. 'Just one or two matters to attend to.'

Venetia drank her tea, puzzled her way through a medical journal lying on the table, got out her notebook and roughly jotted down several matters which would require her attention when they got back, had another look at the journal, did her face, and then wandered round the sombre room, reading with great difficulty the various notices hanging on the notice-board and inspecting the portraits of bygone consultants adorning its walls. She whiled away an hour in this manner, and then went back to her rather uncomfortable chair. She had plenty to think about, but upon reflection she decided not to think too deeply; the future was beginning to loom and she wasn't too happy about it. She closed her eyes and dozed off.

She woke half an hour later. The afternoon had slipped away into evening, and the profound silence of the room was daunting. Perhaps she had been forgotten? She got up and went to open the door on to a silent corridor. There would be no harm in looking round ... She closed the door behind her and walked to the end of the corridor where it met a kind of roundabout of passages. The one to her left looked promising. Besides, there was a noise at the end of it—familiar hospital noise which reassured her. She walked to the end just in time to see Duert coming out of a lift with two white-coated men. He didn't see her, and by the time she had found her surprised voice they had disappeared down yet another corridor.

She must be mad to love a man who could forget her so utterly, it was already all of two hours—he had probably forgotten that he was married. The strong desire to leave the hospital, find a taxi and be driven, at great expense, all the way to Delft was something she managed to suppress. She went back to the consultants' room and sat down again. There was still half a cup of tepid tea in the pot. She drank it, her thoughts on the splendid meal she would eat if, and when, she ever got to Delft.

She went back along the corridor after another half an hour, and kindly Fate allowed Duert to turn into it from another corridor. He stopped short when he saw her, and the look on his face more than repaid her for her long wait. She had never seen him looking other than completely self-possessed, angry or not, but now his handsome features registered the utmost disquiet.

'My dear girl,' he said and took her hands in his. 'I am so sorry...'

'You forgot me,' she observed flatly. 'It's perfectly all right, your work comes first, doesn't it? But if you could spare the time, perhaps you would ask someone to find me a taxi and I'll go back h...to Delft.'

He wasn't the man to smooth over an awkward situation. 'Yes, I did forget you, Venetia. Please, forgive me. I'll take you home now.'

'Will you have to come back?'

'Yes.'

'Then get me a taxi.'

She could have saved her breath. He walked her out of the hospital, ushered her into the Bentley and drove her to Delft, handed her over to Domus, then turned round and drove back to Leiden again.

Domus picked up her cases. He said slowly in Dutch so that she could understand him, 'The professor is a busy man, alas. You will dine at once, *mevrouw*?'

So Venetia tidied her person without much attention and ate her dinner alone. She felt better after that, and went along to the kitchen to see Truus, and then to her room to unpack and take her presents down to the kitchen and, at the same time, make sure that everything was ready for Anneta's return. That done, she went to the drawing-room and sat down with Digby, an open book on her lap, not reading a word.

It was quite late when Duert came home. She had got Truus to cut sandwiches and leave the coffee ready on the Aga, and she went into the hall with the dog as he came in.

He was tired, her loving eyes saw that at a glance. She said quickly, 'Truus made some sandwiches, and there's coffee. I'll fetch it.'

She hadn't expected the mocking smile. 'We mustn't allow this to become a habit, must we? There was no need for you to stay up, Venetia. They look after me very well at the hospital.'

She was a mild-tempered girl, slow to anger, but now she had had enough. 'Oh, good!' she snapped. 'I don't need to concern myself about you any more—so silly of me—there must have been someone running after you, feeding you and seeing that you had clean shirts since the day you were born.' She added loudly, 'And people doing just what you want them to do...' she sniffed '... and then getting forgotten for hours on end.'

He had flung his case down on a chair and crossed the hall towards her, but if she stayed another minute she would burst into tears. She rushed up the staircase and into her room and shut the door.

She undressed in a welter of tears and, quite worn out, got into bed, where she went on weeping into her pillow for quite some time, no longer quite sure why she was crying, but, none the less, most unhappy.

She overslept, and by the time she got downstairs Duert had been gone for some time. There was a note on her plate from him asking her to go with Domus to fetch Anneta from Schiphol, and telling her that he would do his best to get home in good time for dinner that evening.

'Oh, well,' muttered Venetia to herself, 'I had that coming to me, I suppose.'

Anneta's flight was due in at half-past two, and she came through Customs, her arms laden with packages, wearing a leather outfit which was far too hot for the time of year, and which Venetia was sure Duert would frown upon. She flung herself at Venetia with cries of delight, talking all the time while Domus saw to her luggage.

'I have had the most heavenly time,' she declared. 'The party was really something——' she broke off. 'Where's Duert?'

'He couldn't get away—he'll be home as soon as he can this evening.'

They were in the car speeding back to Delft.

'I wouldn't stand for it if I were you,' said Anneta. 'He'll forget he's married if you're not careful.' She sighed. 'I wouldn't put up with it. I need romance not just now and then, but all the time.' She glanced at Venetia. 'Is Duert romantic?'

Venetia felt her cheeks glow. 'I shan't answer that,' she said. 'Now, tell me about your holiday. Did you meet anyone nice?'

'Lots of boys, and one or two men.' Something in her voice made Venetia look at her sharply, but she returned the look guilelessly, going on to give a racy account of her days. It all sounded harmless enough, thought Venetia worriedly, but at the back of her mind was the nagging thought that Anneta wasn't telling her everything.

'And you?' asked Anneta. 'Did you have fun? I've only met Aunt Millicent once. I thought she was pretty dreary.'

'Not a bit of it. We had a lovely time. It's a simply heavenly spot to live in, too. We walked miles.'

Anneta gave a mock sigh. 'I suppose it would be all right for you and Duert—I mean, if you're in love with someone I don't suppose you mind where you are.'

True enough. Venetia agreed with her, and asked if her clothes had been all right.

'Oh, yes, but I bought a few things in Paris. It would have been silly not to, wouldn't it?'

'You found time to shop?'

'Oh, of course,' said Anneta airily, and changed the conversation abruptly.

Duert came home early, to be hugged and kissed by Anneta, and in the flurry of greetings and excited chatter it went unnoticed that he did no more than nod coolly at Venetia, who fielded it back with an icy stare which should have frozen him to the bone, but merely caused him to smile thinly.

On the surface, life settled down to the usual round of pleasant jobs around the house, walks with Digby, shopping and driving lessons. After several more weeks Venetia passed her driving test, so they were able to drive around the country and, rather more cautiously, into den Haag to shop. They had resumed their work at the children's hospital, too, and Venetia was relieved that Anneta seemed willing enough to do her share of the work there. Indeed, after a short time she asked Venetia if she might do an extra afternoon there. 'And no need for you to come in, too,' she declared. 'I know everyone there now, and Wim can drive me in...'

'Well, I could, too...'

'You come and fetch me if you like. Six o'clock outside the main doors. Every Friday.'

So, on one of the rare occasions when Venetia found herself alone with Duert, she was able to tell him that Anneta had settled down very well, and had even volunteered to work extra hours with the children.

'Oh, yes, of course—the children's hospital in Amsterdam. You go there, too, don't you?'

She bit back the tart remark on her tongue. 'Yes,' she told him mildly. 'Anneta will go in with Wim on

Friday, and I'll drive in and fetch her.' She added, 'I can drive now, you know.'

He looked down his nose at her. 'I hadn't forgotten, Venetia.'

But he wasn't always so unresponsive. They were invited out a good deal, not always with Anneta, and then he was exactly as an attentive husband should be. And when from time to time they entertained in their turn he was the perfect host. Sometimes Venetia almost lost heart. The weeks were passing and the warm friendliness they had shared at Selcombe showed no sign of returning. She busied herself running the house efficiently with Truus to guide her, spending a good deal of time with Anneta, and she congratulated herself that at least the girl had changed for the better. Indeed, she was showing a real interest in the children, and when after a week or two she mentioned that she had been asked to work at the convalescent annexe of the hospital Venetia applauded her enthusiasm.

She was taken aback, though, when Duert told them that he would be going over to London in a week's time and they could go with him. 'There's surely some shopping you want to do,' he remarked carelessly, 'and we can do a theatre or two.'

Venetia had known that they would be going, and had even mentioned it to Anneta, but now Anneta flew into a sudden fit of temper. 'But I don't want to go!' she stormed. 'There's so much to do here. You two go—I should think you'd be glad to be on your own. I don't want to miss the tennis, and we were all going to Katwijk to swim...'

'I'll only be there for a couple of weeks,' said Duert mildly, although his eyes were thoughtful. 'In another month or so you'll get all the tennis and swimming you want with your aunt.'

For answer Anneta burst into tears and flew out of the room.

'What did I say wrong?' asked Duert in a voice which dared her to tell him.

So she said quietly, 'Nothing, Duert. I'll talk to her. I'm sure she'll change her mind.'

'I don't want to leave her here on her own.'

'Then I'll stay with her.'

His dark eyes searched her face. 'You would like that? Rather than come to London with me?'

'Oh, no. I want to go with you.' She had spoken eagerly, but his questioning look brought her up short. 'The garden will be in full bloom,' she said the first thing which came into her head, 'and the Heath will be lovely. Besides, Anneta and I can shop.'

He said silkily, 'Just for a moment I thought you might have another reason.' He got up and crossed over to the door. 'I have some work to do—I'm sure that you'll do your best with Anneta.'

She watched him go. It seemed to her that he avoided being with her for as much of the time as he could, and yet at Salcombe they had spent their days happily walking and talking. Perhaps because there had been no one else, she thought unhappily.

Presently she went upstairs and knocked on Anneta's door. She was bidden to go in, and to her surprise she found Anneta all smiles.

She got up off her bed and flung her arm around Venetia's shoulders. 'Darling Venetia, I'm sorry I was so cross, and I can't think why. I'd love to go to Hampstead with you both. We can shop, can't we? And go for walks on the Heath, and I've friends, too, I can go and see them.'

'Yes, of course you can, dear. I'm so glad you've changed your mind, for Duert was disappointed...'

'Oh, well, now he can cheer up. When are we going?'

'I don't know exactly—I expect he'll tell us as soon as he's got his theatre lists made up. I think we'll be gone for at least a fortnight, perhaps three weeks. Even so, you'll still have time to visit all your friends here before you go.'

'I hope I'll like it in the States—all my friends—I shall miss them.'

'You'll make new ones. Besides, it only takes a few hours to fly over these days.'

'I'll come back with a multimillionaire,' said Anneta, and giggled.

'I dare say there are plenty to choose from,' said Venetia, 'but do remember that money isn't half as important as being happy.'

'I'd be unhappy without it,' said Anneta. 'Wouldn't you?'

'Well, no, but then, you see, for quite a few years before I married Duert I hadn't any money—at least, only just enough to get by.'

'Would you have married Duert if he had had no money?'

'Oh, yes, and when you fall in love you'll see what I mean.' She got up. 'Are you coming downstairs to tell Duert that you are going with us?'

They went a week later, and Duert expected to be at St Jude's for at least two weeks. Anneta had become quite enthusiastic about it, and had written to several of her friends in London arranging meetings. 'You won't mind?' she wanted to know. 'They're all old friends, and Duert knows them, and it'll be a chance to say goodbye to them.' She had danced off to go through her wardrobe, ready to pack, and Venetia had heaved a sigh of relief. The girl had changed enormously—ready to fall in with Duert's wishes, and adamant, too, that she should continue to go to the children's hospital in Amsterdam until the very last day before they were to leave Holland.

Venetia had cried off. There was too much to see to in the house, and last-minute phone calls to make, but half-way through the afternoon she remembered that she had forgotten to tell her teacher that her Dutch lessons would have to be put off for a few weeks. She owed money for her lessons, too, so she got out the car and drove into Delft, found the flat where the old Mijnheer de Wolke lived, explained it all to him, paid her debts and drank a cup of tea with him and his wife, and then hurried back to the car. She was getting in when she paused to stare down the street. She was parked on Oude Delft, a tree-lined street running beside the main canal, and as usual it was crowded, but ahead of her, on the other side of the canal, she thought she had seen Anneta. Even as she looked a party of cyclists blocked out her view, and when they had passed there was no sign of anyone even faintly resembling Anneta.

Venetia got into the car and drove home. It couldn't have been Anneta—she was in Amsterdam. There were, after all, any number of pretty girls like her, and why would she be in Delft, anyway? She allowed common sense to take over, but it didn't quite blot out a vague uneasiness.

She finished her packing and went out into the garden. Duert had said that he would be late home, and Anneta had promised to be back in time for tea. A friend was giving her a lift, she had told Venetia when she had suggested that she should fetch her. And sure enough, Venetia hadn't been outside for more

than half an hour when a car drove up, deposited
Anneta at the gates and drove off.

Anneta ran to meet her. 'Hello,' she called. 'See
how punctual I am. Such a busy day, too—all those
children and the noise...'

'You're tired, dear? We'll have tea. Duert's going
to be late home.'

'I'll finish my packing after tea. Have you been
busy?'

Venetia said, 'Not particularly. I had to go to
Delft—I forgot to tell Mijnheer de Wolke that I'd be
away for a bit, and I hadn't paid him.' She glanced
at Anneta. 'So silly, I thought I saw you there on Oude
Delft—you with a man.'

The change of expression on Anneta's face was so
swift that she decided she had imagined it. 'Me? In
Delft? Darling Venetia, how could it have been me?'

'I know. I said I was silly. Let's have tea, shall we?'

They waited dinner for Duert, and the meal was
eaten in the highest spirits. Anneta was at the top of
her form, teasing Duert, planning shopping trips with
Venetia, going into endless detail about the friends
she intended visiting while they were at Hampstead.
She skipped off to her room soon after they had had
coffee, and Duert picked up the post which had been
put by his chair. 'You'll forgive me if I see to this lot?
I won't have time in the morning. I can dictate the
replies and Juffrouw Floos can see to them after we
have gone.'

Juffrouw Floos was his secretary, a formidable lady,
who spoke Dutch to Venetia very slowly and clearly
and expected to be answered in the same language.
Venetia was a little scared of her.

She nodded cheerfully, for she had expected him to
do just that the moment Anneta had gone. When he

had closed the door quietly behind him she picked up her tapestry work once more, her unhappy thoughts keeping pace with her flying needle.

She was her usual composed self in the morning, making sure that everything was just so before they left while Duert took Digby for a quick walk. Anneta had come down to breakfast punctually for once, and had gone upstairs to check that she had everything she would need and phone Mieke. 'Just to say goodbye...'

'But you'll see her before you go off to America,' protested Venetia.

'Darling Venetia, of course I shall, but I forgot to ask her the name of that perfume she asked me to get from Harrods.'

She skipped away, the very picture of content.

Their journey to Hampstead went smoothly, but travelling with Duert, Venetia had already discovered, was always without worries of any sort. And it was delightful to be welcomed by the Todds, to have one's bags taken away and unpacked and a tea-tray set in the drawing-room without having to raise either a finger or a voice. Truly, such a comfortable life was bliss, yet she would have exchanged every moment of it if she had Duert's love in its place.

She saw very little of him—at breakfast for half an hour and at dinner in the evening, but Anneta was always with them, so that even if she had known what to say she had no chance to say it. But talk they must sooner or later, she decided; the future without the need to mother Anneta was looming rapidly. In the meanwhile she did her best, presenting a serene front when Anneta was there, playing the part of a contented, happy wife.

She had her small rewards, for Anneta, watching her bidding Duert goodbye at breakfast, said thoughtfully, 'You know, it has been very revealing, watching you and Duert. There must be something worth having—when you are really happily married, I mean. Just being together whenever you can. Almost all my friends' parents are divorced or live their own lives. I shall take care whom I marry.' She giggled suddenly. 'But I intend to have fun first.'

Her opinion was endorsed by Duert that evening after she had gone to bed and just for once he stayed in the drawing-room for a while, watching Venetia at her tapestry. 'Anneta is a changed girl,' he told her. 'You have worked a miracle, Venetia, just by being you. It has been a very worthwhile arrangement, don't you agree?'

She agreed. Now was perhaps the time to have a talk. She marshalled her thoughts carefully, and had them nicely sorted out when he got up abruptly. 'I must ring Arthur. I'll see you at breakfast.'

She nodded, speechless with disappointment.

She and Anneta spent several days shopping. There seemed no end to the clothes she would need in the States even though, Anneta being Anneta, she would buy another complete wardrobe when she got there. But after the first week she started her rounds of visits to her friends. Lunch parties, morning coffee, visits to some special boutique—almost every day was filled, although she was always back home before Duert returned from the hospital.

Venetia felt uneasy, although she wasn't sure why she should be, but when she mentioned Anneta's endless engagements to Duert he remarked casually that she had any number of friends all over the place. 'As long as she is enjoying herself,' he added.

That was obvious, for she returned from her visits bright-eyed and excited, ready to give Venetia rambling accounts of the various friends she had met. It was towards the end of the second week that Venetia, having occasion to go to Liberty for silks for her embroidery, wandered out of the shop to stand for a moment idly looking around her. It was a splendid day, and warm, and the street was crowded with tourists. She thought how lucky she was to be living in the peace and quiet of Hampstead. She remembered that Mrs Todd had asked her to get the special Parma ham the professor liked if she happened to be in town, and she hailed a taxi to take her to Harrods. She had to wait a few minutes, for the traffic was thick, but suddenly there was a brief emptiness and exactly opposite to her on the far pavement stood Anneta, her arm tucked into that of a tall, thin man, young and smartly dressed, who even as Venetia gaped bent to kiss Anneta, who flung her other arm around him, laughing. It was then that she saw Venetia, who turned away and got into the waiting taxi, sitting like a poker in the back, her mind in a whirl. She said 'Harrods, please,' and sat back, and then started to think. Anneta's visits and tea parties were probably a blind, and perhaps it *had* been her in Delft—and who was the man? And what on earth was Duert going to say?

CHAPTER NINE

VENETIA wandered round the food hall at Harrods, looking at the numerous delicacies with an unseeing eye, grappling with the problem of Anneta, and presently going back into the Brompton Road again, the Parma ham quite forgotten, and making her way in a haphazard fashion by bus back to Hampstead. Once back home she went into the garden and sat down to think. How deeply was Anneta involved? she wondered. Or was she involved at all? Was it a chance encounter? She thought not, and now she came to think about it she had seen the man before, at a coffee party Anneta had given in Delft. She had joined them for a few minutes, and there had been perhaps a dozen girls and young men there. She hadn't wanted Anneta to feel that she was prying on her friends, so she had said a general good morning and gone away again. But he had been there, she was quite sure of that. So why was he here in London? He must have followed Anneta, which meant that it wasn't just a casual flirtation.

She heard a car draw up presently, and Anneta's voice as she went into the house, and she got up and went indoors and upstairs to the girl's room. They would have to talk, and the sooner the better.

She tapped on the door and went in, and Anneta turned to face her, on her face a mixture of defiance and fright.

'If you tell Duert I shall die,' she declared wildly. 'I'll kill myself.'

'How can I tell Duert anything when I don't know much myself?' asked Venetia in a quiet voice. 'But I do think that you should tell me, dear. Will you talk about it?'

Anneta flung out her arms dramatically. 'I'm in love—and it is not your kind of love, so staid and proper, but exciting and such fun...'

'More fun, perhaps, because it was secret?'

'Well, yes. You never knew, did you? Never guessed?'

Venetia sat down on the bed. 'I think I guessed... You were suddenly so enthusiastic about working at the hospital and I wondered why, but I hoped that you would tell me. And then I saw you in Delft, didn't I?'

'Yes. Oh, but we've been meeting for ages—ever since I was in Paris.'

'So that's why you didn't want to come here with us—because you thought you wouldn't be able to see him?'

Anneta laughed. 'That's right, Venetia. But, you see, I telephoned him and he followed us here.'

'Have you been to any of these friends you were supposed to be meeting?'

She was given a scornful look. 'Of course not.'

'And now tell me why I shouldn't tell Duert? He is your guardian for another few weeks.'

Anneta burst into tears. 'I'll kill myself if you do, I mean that. He is kind to me, he has looked after me for a long time, and I must have unsettled his life. He is strict, but only because he is too old to understand what being in love means. Why, even with you he is so—so unexcited, but perhaps you like that.' She flung herself at Venetia. 'Darling Venetia, please, please don't tell him. You are so kind and good, and do you not see? I want him to remember me as a nice,

well-brought-up girl.' She peered at Venetia, the
picture of a woebegone child. 'I don't know if he ever
told you, but I wasn't always good at school in
Switzerland. I liked to go out with boys, and sometimes I would escape, but I was caught and Duert was
so angry. I promised I would never behave badly
again...'

'And you've broken that promise.'

There was a fresh flood of tears. 'Venetia, darling
Venetia, if I promise you faithfully that I'll not see
Jan again, will you promise not to tell Duert? I will
be so good, truly I will.' She peeped from under her
lashes. 'I'll go everywhere with you, and when we go
back to Delft you shall come everywhere with me. It's
only a few weeks now before I go away. Besides, we'll
be so busy getting ready for my party.' She began to
cry again. 'If Duert finds out he won't give me a
birthday party. I can't be eighteen without a party.'

Venetia had a fleeting memory of being eighteen,
celebrating it with Granny with a small iced cake and
a bottle of sherry. There had been a letter on that day,
too, offering her a place at one of the minor uni-
versities. She had refused it because, even with a grant,
it had been beyond Granny's means. She had started
her job as a doctor's receptionist the very next day,
and had been contented and grateful for her weekly
pay-packet. She sighed silently. Anneta had had a different upbringing from her own, and she shouldn't
allow her own disappointments to colour her
judgement. She said prosaically, 'If you will give me
your solemn word not to see this—Jan again, and to
do all you can to please Duert, then I promise never
to tell him.'

Anneta flung her arms round her neck. 'You dear,
kind Venetia, I promise. I'll be good, and I'll do
everything to make Duert pleased with me.' She

paused. 'There's just one thing—may I write to Jan and tell him that I'm not going to see him again, and that he's not to write or phone?' And when Venetia hesitated, 'I'll show you the letter.'

'Very well. Better do it now. Then do your face—Duert has very sharp eyes—and come down for tea.'

She went along to her own room and sat down before the looking-glass and inspected her face. She would have liked a good weep herself—more than that, she wanted above all things to fling herself into Duert's arms and tell him all about it, instead of which she must present the calm, ordinary face he had come to expect when he returned home. She set to work and, since she was so pale, applied a trace of blusher to her cheeks. A distinct improvement, she considered.

Anneta came downstairs presently, and over tea handed Venetia the letter she had written. It was a model of rectitude, and Venetia handed it back with a satisfied nod. Anneta slipped it into the envelope she had in her hand and stuck it down. 'I'll post it after tea,' she said with just the right touch of sadness.

Duert got home at about six o'clock, and to Venetia's loving eyes he looked desperately tired. 'You've had a busy day?' she asked as he crossed the hall.

'Not so much bad as hot and long. The last case took five hours.'

'But it was successful . . . ?'

'Yes, so far.' He smiled at her suddenly. 'I forgot that you are interested; Anneta hates anything to do with surgery—or did—but since you have been here she has at least taken an interest in the children. A feather in your cap.'

He started up the staircase. 'I'll be ten minutes. I could do with a drink when I come down.'

She poured him a whisky and went and sat down by the open window. She felt nervous, although she told herself that she had nothing to be nervous about; Anneta had promised and Duert need never know. All the same, she hated deceiving him. She got up and nipped across the room to peer into the magnificent chimney-piece mirror. She looked much as usual; she must try not to blush...

She became aware that he was standing behind her, watching her in the mirror, his gaze so intent and thoughtful, and she felt her cheeks go warm. Duert, studying her face, wondered why she looked so guilty and why she had needed to use blusher. He asked in a deceptively gentle voice, 'What's wrong, Venetia?'

Her voice came out in an anxious squeak. 'Wrong? There's nothing wrong.' She managed a rather shrill laugh. 'I've poured your drink. It's on the table by your chair.'

'Thank you, Venetia.'

He bent and kissed her, and she said in a wispy voice, 'Oh, why did you do that? There is no need. Anneta isn't here...'

'One must keep one's hand in,' he said blandly, and went to sit down, but paused on the way. 'Won't you have a drink?'

And when she nodded he poured her a glass of sherry and brought it to her. 'After a hard day's work I find it most relaxing,' he said, and kissed her again just as Anneta came in.

She danced up to them and gave Duert a hug. 'It must be delightful to come home to a dear little wife like Venetia,' she declared. 'What a pity you aren't home more often.'

'Indeed it is,' he agreed gravely, 'but I've given myself some time off tomorrow. I've got tickets for the *Phantom of the Opera*, and I thought we might dine out first.' He spoke to Anneta, but he looked at Venetia.

She said in her quiet way, 'That will be delightful, Duert. Will you be home really early for tea?'

'Yes, I think so. You'll both be here?'

'Yes, of course. We're going to have a quiet day and spend an hour or two in the pool.' She looked at Anneta. 'Aren't we, dear?'

'Yes—we'll have a picnic lunch there, shall we? Mrs Todd will make sandwiches. Duert, can't you come home for lunch?'

He shook his head. 'No, I've an outpatients' clinic until one o'clock, but I'll be able to get away during the afternoon.'

The evening passed without incident, and if Duert was surprised at the almost feverish way Venetia kept a trivial conversation going, and her look of unhappiness when she thought herself to be unobserved, he said nothing.

He took them to Le Gavroche the following evening, explaining that it was by way of being a farewell dinner party in London. 'At least, for the time being,' he added, 'although I dare say we shall celebrate again before you leave.'

Venetia hadn't known where they were going, but she had seen Todd laying out the professor's dinnerjacket in his room. She rooted through her wardrobe and decided upon a long-sleeved taffeta dress, the colour of her eyes, cut with a full skirt and a ruffled chiffon bodice. She knew she had chosen well when she saw the look of approval on Duert's face, and she ate with appetite her smoked salmon followed by chicken Bresse with a white sauce with mustard and cream and white wine added, rounding off these delights with a *glace praline*. They reached the theatre with minutes to spare, and she sat enthralled for the rest of the evening. She forgot Anneta—she even forgot Duert from time to time—her gaze fixed steadily upon the stage, unaware that his attention was entirely taken up by the study of her face.

During the next few days Anneta was a model of docile behaviour, evincing no desire to go off on her own, helping with the flowers around the house, going to the shops with Venetia, and spending long hours by the pool. Almost too good to be true, only there was no reason to be suspicious.

Duert came and went. Venetia sensed that he was avoiding her, although he was thoughtful for her comfort and quite prepared to be regaled with their day's happenings when he got home. He looked tired. More than tired, she decided worriedly; he had something on his mind, but somehow there was never the right moment to ask him.

Another week went by, and they returned to Delft, where he was at once engulfed in a backlog of work, both at the hospitals and at his consulting rooms, so Venetia and Anneta were left to make the plans for the birthday party. Duert had told them to do what they liked, within reason, so invitations had been sent out to all Anneta's friends as well as a number of older guests, and since almost all of them had accepted the plans could be put into effect. Truus had consented to having the caterers in, although she had insisted on making the birthday cake. A marquee was to be erected in the garden behind the drawing-room and, at Anneta's insistence, two bands had been engaged—one for the more staid guests, the other a group of her choosing. She chose the food, too, since it was her party, and then bore Venetia off to den Haag to buy suitable dresses for such an important occasion.

She set her heart on an outrageous dress in black satin, very short, very tight and guaranteed to send

Duert into one of his coldly bland moods. Venetia pointed out that Anneta wouldn't be able to dance in comfort, however wonderfully it fitted while she was standing still. Moreover, she hinted it was rather youthful for a girl of Anneta's age. With guile and the help of a quick-thinking saleslady, she pointed out the advantages of an electric-blue dress with a ruched bodice and a very full, short skirt. 'Dance around and you'll see what I mean,' she suggested. 'You could get a pair of those Italian slippers . . .'

Satisfied at last, Anneta said, 'Now you, Venetia. Something gorgeous—scarlet or emerald-green . . .'

But Venetia knew what she wanted. With quiet insistence she had her way, and returned home with a misty-blue dress with enormous puff sleeves and a wide sweeping skirt, and a pair of matching shoes with diamond buckles.

She was up early on the morning of the party. The caterers would be coming after breakfast, and she and Truus would have to decide on what meals they would have. Duert, breakfasting with her, thought it unlikely that he would get home before tea, which would make it easy for Truus, for she and Anneta would need only a light lunch. 'But you'll be home for tea?' she asked.

He looked up from the letter he was reading. 'Oh, yes, as far as I know. You seem to have organised everything very well. You're not too tired?'

'Me? Not in the least.' Her eyes searched his face. 'Afterwards, Duert, can we have a talk?'

'When Anneta has gone, yes, of course.' He smiled suddenly at her, and her heart tripped up. 'We so seldom have time to talk, you and I. And there is a great deal I want to say to you.'

He got up and gathered up his letters, ready to leave. He paused by her chair and bent to kiss her, and for a moment she thought that he was going to say something more, but he went through the door without a word.

The day went in a flash and Venetia, consulting with the caterers, arranging the great bowls and vases of flowers, making sure that no stone had been left unturned in her efforts to make the party a success, saw little of Anneta. Only when Domus came to say that lunch was waiting did she appear suddenly in the small room where they were to have their meal.

'I've been washing my hair and doing my nails,' she volunteered before Venetia could speak, 'and reading all the cards I've had. I'm dying to open my presents...'

'Well, it will be more fun when Duert's here. He's coming home for tea, so you'll have heaps of time to see them all before we have to dress.'

'I wonder what you've given me? Did you choose it together?'

'No, but we agreed about it, and Duert got it.' Which was only partly true, for he had shown her the pearl necklace he had bought, remarking that it was from both of them. 'And I've ordered flowers, of course,' he had added.

They had arrived that morning—a glorious bouquet of roses and orchids and carnations—and Venetia had thought wistfully that it must be wonderful to be given extravagant bouquets by someone who loved you. It would be even more wonderful to be given even a humble bunch of daisies, if Duert offered them with love...

Duert came home, and over tea the presents were opened and admired and the necklace fastened round Anneta's youthful neck. She ran to admire it in the looking-glass, turning this way and that. 'It's beautiful. Shall you wear your pearls this evening, Venetia?'

'Oh, yes.' She didn't add that she had nothing else worthy of her new gown.

She went downstairs well before the first guests would arrive and, with Digby as escort, did a round of the house to make sure that everything was just as it should be. She ended up in the drawing-room, its furniture arranged around the walls, the wood-block floor cleared for dancing. The older guests might prefer to dance indoors or sit around gossiping. She hoped that she had done everything properly—it was the first big party she had organised, and she was desperately anxious to please Duert.

He had followed her silently and she jumped round as he spoke.

'Everything seems to be exactly right, Venetia. You have hidden talents I was not well aware of.' He took her hands and held her arms wide. 'That is a particularly fetching frock. I hope you persuaded Anneta to buy something just as charming.'

She had gone pink, but she answered prosaically, 'Well, it was a bit difficult—she had set her heart on very tight black satin—but I think you'll like her choice. Here she is now.'

Anneta looked quite lovely. The dress suited her, and she had taken great pains with her face and hair. 'You will take the States by storm,' Duert assured her gravely, 'and certainly you will be the belle of your ball.'

'I do look nice, don't I?' said Anneta complacently. 'What about Venetia? Don't you think she looks nice, too?'

'Very nice. I hear the first of our guests...'

It was obvious from the start that the party was going to be a success. The house filled, and then spilled its guests out into the marquee to dance and eat the food Anneta had chosen with such care. The din was deafening, with the band of Anneta's choice belting out the latest hits, and the younger guests crowding on to the floor to fling themselves around to its beat. It looked great fun, reflected Venetia, going back to the drawing-room to circle the room with a sober colleague of Duert's.

The band finished the waltz it was playing, and they paused by the open french windows. The gardens had been festooned with coloured lights and Venetia admired them, half listening to her companion's opinion of the country's politics, but suddenly she stiffened. Almost at the end of the lawns sweeping away from the house there was a small ornamental fountain, and standing by it were two people. Anneta, and, unless she was mistaken, the man Jan.

Venetia laid an urgent hand on her companion's arm. 'Forgive me, there is something I must attend to at once.'

She gave him a smile and he patted her hand. 'My dear lady, you have performed miracles. I can forgive you anything.'

She sped down the path, and Duert, watching from the other end of the room, excused himself without haste from the elderly cousin he had been talking to and strolled over to the french windows. He said casually, 'Ah, Cor—I thought I saw my wife with you. I wanted a word with her, the speeches, you know...'

'A charming girl. You are a lucky man, Duert. Yes, she was with me, but she said that there was something urgent she simply had to attend to—a most efficient woman.' He nodded towards the gardens. 'She went towards the fountain, I believe.'

The professor wandered outside. 'I'll see if I can find her.'

He went unhurriedly along the path, and then stopped when he saw the three people standing by the fountain. It was quite quiet in the garden, and he could hear them talking easily enough.

Anneta was standing a little apart, and it was Venetia's voice which came to him so clearly.

'You promised,' she was saying, her voice a little shrill either with fright or temper. 'Why are you here? What is the professor going to say if he finds out——?'

'A great deal, I should imagine,' said Duert silkily.

Venetia wheeled round to face him, but it was Anneta who spoke. 'Duert! Oh, thank heaven you've come.' She ran to him and took his arm. 'I tried to stop Venetia, truly I did. I didn't want you to discover them. I told her that you'd be furious. And it's partly Jan's fault for coming here when he promised her that he wouldn't. They've been meeting for weeks—even in London.' She gave a little sob. 'I love you both so much. You must forgive her. I'm sure it's just infatuation...'

He gave her his handkerchief. 'Dry your eyes, Anneta, and go and look after your guests. You, too, Venetia.' He sounded almost placid, but neither of them disobeyed him. Anneta ran on ahead without looking at Venetia, and she, after one fruitless attempt to speak to him, turned and walked back to the house. Later, when the guests had all gone, she would be able to explain...

The rest of the evening was a confusion of noise and music and people laughing and talking, with the cake being cut and speeches being made. She listened to Duert saying how he would miss Anneta, how she had been like a daughter to him, and how proud he was of her. She remembered then that she had promised Anneta never to tell Duert about Jan. But

Anneta had broken her own promise and, worse, she had given Duert a completely false idea about what had happened. She could only suppose that Anneta had lost her head when she saw Duert, and had said the first thing that had entered her head. Venetia prayed silently for the evening to end so that she could explain and Anneta could own up.

There had, of course, been no chance of talking to her. They had stood together while the cake was being cut, but she had avoided Venetia's eye, and although Duert had behaved impeccably, and he had smiled and said all the right things, his eyes had been dark granite.

When finally the last guest had gone, Anneta had rushed off to her room without a word, and when Venetia had taken her courage in both hands and asked Duert, 'Could we talk? Just for a moment?' he had answered her blandly.

'Surely it's rather late for that, Venetia? I shan't be at home tomorrow; I have to go to Groningen.' He gave her a bleak smile. 'I must congratulate you upon the success of the party. Don't let me keep you, you must be tired.'

She studied his stony face—now was the moment to go. It was not the right time to get things sorted out. She said goodnight and went to her room and got ready for bed, and then on an impulse went along to Anneta's room. But there was no answer to her knock, and the door was locked.

There was no sign of Anneta at breakfast. Everything was quiet after the brisk packing up done by the caterers, and Truus and the maids had already set the house to rights. Venetia went along to the kitchen to talk about the meals and exchange gossip with Truus about the ladies' dresses and the party.

'It'll be quiet without Miss Anneta,' remarked Truus in her slow, basic Dutch so that Venetia could understand. 'Tomorrow she goes, doesn't she? Quite a different life where she's going to live, I dare say. Shall I send one of the girls up to wake her, *mevrouw*?'

'Let her sleep, Truus. I'm going into the garden with Digby.'

She was sitting on a little rustic seat at the very end of the garden when Anneta joined her. Venetia wished her good morning and said did she want her breakfast.

Anneta shook her head. 'Venetia, I'm so sorry about last night. Truly I am. I really meant to keep my promise, but Jan thought it would be such fun to meet in secret under Duert's nose and right in the middle of my party. Only when I saw him standing there I lost my head. You see, I do want Duert to remember me as he thinks I am. He would be so angry if he thought I was—fooling around—and he doesn't like Jan. In fact, he forbade me to see him, oh, years ago now, while I was still at school. But when I saw him again in Paris...'

She paused and looked at Venetia, who didn't say a word. 'I'll be gone tomorrow,' she said in a wheedling voice, 'and you can explain then.'

'No, I can't. I promised I wouldn't say anything to him, or have you forgotten that as well?'

'You're angry with me.' Anneta sounded on the brink of tears. 'And just when I'm leaving here, and perhaps we won't see each other again ever.'

'It only takes a few hours to fly the Atlantic. I'm quite sure you'll visit us.'

'Yes, well, I don't suppose Duert really minds about you and Jan. After all, he must know that you love him. You do love him? Don't you?' Just for a moment she sounded anxious.

'When you think about it,' said Venetia soberly, 'that makes it much worse, doesn't it? What happened to Jan?—for of course you will have phoned him...'

'Well, yes, I did. Just to say goodbye—he was fun.' She gave a nervous giggle. 'I asked him what Duert had said to him, and he said he didn't wish to talk about it. Venetia, you won't say anything to Duert until I've gone, and then only if you really have to?'

'I keep my promises,' said Venetia, and thought how priggish that sounded.

'I knew you'd understand. I adore Duert, you know. I know he's almost old, and not in the least exciting, but he's been like a father to me, you see. And I'm sure he doesn't really mind about you and Jan.'

'But there's nothing to mind. I've not spoken more than half a dozen words to the man.'

'Well, there you are, then. So there's nothing to worry about, is there?'

Venetia saw that the conversation was pointless. She got up. 'Truus will have made the coffee,' she said tonelessly.

Duert didn't come back until long after they had gone to bed. Venetia, lying awake, heard his quiet tread as he went to his room. And in the morning they would drive to Schiphol and see Anneta on to the plane. Even if she had wanted to tell him all about it, there was going to be no opportunity.

No one would have known that there was anything wrong the next morning. Anneta talked non-stop, bubbling over with excitement, only every now and then when there was a pause in the talk she would glance anxiously at Venetia and then plunge into more chatter. And as for Duert, he was exactly as he always was, sitting calmly behind the wheel, joking with Anneta and coldly polite to Venetia. Not a word was uttered about the incident at the fountain, but why should it be? she reflected, sitting at the back of the car with Digby. As far as Duert was concerned, there was no need to say another word about it to Anneta, who had, after all, done her best to keep him from knowing about Venetia and Jan. Venetia allowed a number of unkind thoughts to take over, and then dismissed them. The harm had been done.

They waited until they saw the plane airborne. Somehow Venetia had gone through the miserable business of saying goodbye, hoping until the very last minute that Anneta would confess. But she didn't, and now, sitting beside Duert in the car, going back to Delft, Venetia gave up that hope.

After several miles in silence, she said quite quietly, 'I should like to talk to you when we get back, Duert.'

'Ah, yes—you have plans for the future? I'm afraid I must go straight to Leiden, but I'll be back for dinner. Afterwards, perhaps?'

And that was all they said.

She had no plans, but it seemed that she was expected to have some. To go away for a while, perhaps, a kind of cooling-off period, and afterwards they would be able to talk sensibly. They parted politely in the hall, and when he had gone she ate a few mouthfuls of lunch and went into the garden with Digby. She loved the garden and the house, and she loved the house at Hampstead, too, but without Duert they meant nothing. To go right away seemed the answer, but where should she go? The answer popped into her head, and she said out loud, 'Of course, how silly of me. Aunt Millicent—if she will have me. And if Duert wants to see me, he'll know where I am.'

She felt better after that, so that when he got home she was able to greet him with her usual serenity and carry on a conversation during dinner. Only afterwards, sitting with him in the drawing-room, she found it hard to start. Presently she said, 'Duert, could we have a talk?'

He put down his coffee-cup and sat back in his chair. He said suavely, 'By all means, Venetia,' and glanced at his watch. He wasn't going to help her.

She said tartly, 'I won't keep you long.' She threw him a look of such irritation that he frowned a little. 'I have never tried to keep you from whatever you wanted to do, and I'm not going to now.'

He was staring at her rather too intently for her peace of mind. 'I am aware that I have been a neglectful husband—it is only recently that I have realised that.'

'Well, never mind that now,' said Venetia, intent on getting matters over and done with. 'I should like to go away, just for a little while, while we decide— while *you* decide what you want. Do you think that Aunt Millicent would have me for a few days? I have nowhere else to go.'

'Certainly you may go if you wish to. But will you not tell me exactly what has been happening these last months? If I have neglected you, then I am sorry, Venetia, although I believe that when we married I made it clear that my work was important to me. But I had begun to hope that things might change between us. I see that I was wrong. This Jan is a young man . . . Will you tell me about him?'

'There's nothing to tell—nothing I want to say . . .'

'In that case, we'll say no more, only he's not worth a row of pins, my dear, and I would not want to see you hurt.'

She managed not to cry. She hadn't expected him to say that.

He got to his feet. 'I'll arrange for you to travel. Let me see—the day after tomorrow? Wim can drive you to Schiphol. I'm going to Paris tomorrow, and I shall be away for a few days—just as well... I'm sorry this has happened.' He stopped by her chair. 'I had begun to hope that you liked me rather more than you used to, and as for me—I've fallen in love with you, Venetia.'

He had gone out of the room before she could gather her wits, and even when her first instinct was to run after him she remembered that he still believed that she had been having an affair with Jan. How could she ask him to forgive her for something she hadn't done?

She went to bed presently, and lay awake until the first early morning light before falling into troubled sleep, to wake with the disturbing thought that she had no idea of how she was to get to Salcombe. She wasn't sure if she had enough money, and she would need to go to London and take another train to Kingsbridge and a taxi from there, but by the time she went downstairs for her breakfast she had a headache.

She had worried for nothing. There was an envelope by her plate with a thick bundle of notes inside and a brief letter. A late morning flight on the following day had been arranged for her, and Wim would drive her to Schiphol, where she could collect her ticket. Todd would meet her at Heathrow, and she was to spend the night at Hampstead; he would drive her down to Salcombe in the morning. Aunt Millicent was expecting her.

The note was a model of clarity, like instructions concerning a patient, and there was no mention of meeting again. She held back tears with an effort, quite unable to believe that the writer of such an austere missive could possibly be in love with her. She drank her coffee, called Digby and took him for his walk, her thoughts running round inside her head like

mice in a cage, so that her headache became un-
bearable. All the same, she reminded herself, the day
had to be got through. She went to the kitchen, made
arrangements with Truus, relieved to find that Duert
had already told her and Domus that she was going
to his aunt's for a short rest after all the excitement
of getting Anneta away. 'And you'll soon be back,'
said Truus comfortably. 'The professor will be lonely.
It's a relief to know that Anneta arrived safely, isn't
it?'

Venetia agreed. She would have phoned Duert, of
course. She went to her room and started to pack a
few clothes. If she took her time over it, the day might
go more quickly...

There was no message from Duert before she left
the next day, and she supposed she had been foolish
to expect one. As she wished everyone goodbye she
wondered when she would see them again, and the
sight of Digby, ears drooping, was almost more than
she could bear. She turned to wave as Wim drove her
away, and Truus waved back.

'There's something wrong,' she said to Domus. 'I
feel it in my bones.'

The journey went smoothly, and since Wim saw her
off and Todd met her she had nothing to worry her.
She was given a warm welcome by Mrs Todd, and no
one asked any questions. Lulled by the Todds'
kindness, she slept all night. They set off early the
next day and, since it was a fine morning and there
wasn't a great deal of traffic, they made good time.
Todd was a kindly man and a good driver; she sat
beside him and carried on an undemanding conversation about the party and Anneta's departure and
her life in Delft. Neither of them mentioned Duert,
she because she was trying not to think of him, and
he because the professor had warned him that his wife

had had an exhausting few weeks and needed a change of scene.

Aunt Millicent, sitting placidly knitting in her drawing-room, appeared not to have moved since Venetia had last seen her, although she had, as a concession to the seasons, changed her blouse and skirt for a twin set and tweeds. Her welcome was warm and unquestioning. Venetia was given tea and Meg's scones, and told to go and unpack her things. 'And, as it is still light, you might like a stroll along the sands,' suggested Aunt Millicent.

Why not? thought Venetia, getting out of her clothes, having a shower and putting on a Marks and Spencer's skirt and a rather elderly cotton sweater. Todd was to stay the night—she glanced out of the window, and wondered why he hadn't put the car away...

The professor, with the second of his lectures in Paris cancelled by his own wish, got back home within hours of Venetia's departure. He had behaved abominably, and now he was reaping his reward. He had allowed his pride and jealousy to swamp common sense and, above all, his love. He came into the house like a whirlwind, told Domus to pack a bag, ate the meal Truus insisted upon setting before him, and booked a passage on a night ferry. Arthur was treated to a terse series of instructions. 'And I don't know when I'll be back,' said the professor, in a voice which defied his registrar to ask questions.

He was within an hour of leaving the house when Anneta telephoned. She sounded tearful and burst into a wild speech when he told her that Venetia wasn't there. 'But I must speak to her,' wailed Anneta. 'Duert, I've been so wicked, it was me, not her...'

'Supposing you start from the beginning,' said Duert in Dutch, 'and tell me exactly what is worrying you.'

It all came pouring out, a muddle of half-finished sentences, appeals for forgiveness, and regret that she had blamed Venetia, who was an angel. 'And you're angry,' finished Anneta, 'and that's why I did it, so that you wouldn't be angry, and now you are.'

He reassured her in his calm way. 'I'm on my way to join Venetia now,' he said soothingly, 'and you don't need to worry any more. Only don't entangle with any more Jans, my dear.'

He left soon after. He had a long drive ahead of him, but Venetia would be at the end of it, and that was all that mattered. He would be in England within a few hours, and could drive through the remainder of the night...

The beach was empty, and the quiet sea washed the edge of the cove with a soothing swish. Venetia wandered across the sand towards the rocks, her head empty of everything but one wish: that Duert could be there with her. She gained the rocks on the further side and stopped to look around her. Duert was sitting on a rock watching her. Her heart jerked against her ribs, and her voice came out in a squeak. 'Duert, how did you get here?'

'By car.' He got up and came towards her. 'I went back home because I had to see you, and before I left Anneta telephoned. My darling Venetia, why didn't you tell me?'

'I promised.' She added with some spirit, 'Anyway, you were so angry.'

'Angry? I could have wrung that man's neck. The thought of him touching you ...'

'But he didn't. But you didn't need to come just to tell me that.'

'No, I came to tell you what you already know.' He held out a hand and she caught the sparkle of amethysts, the sheen of pearls and the delicate green of the entwined leaves. 'I'm in love with you, and this is to prove it, my darling girl. I think that I have always loved you, from the moment I first set eyes on you. Perhaps I didn't know that when I bought this necklace, I knew only that it was right for you, shy and gentle like that long-ago bride. I am not sure how it happened, but you have become part of my life, and if I ask you to come back to me, and perhaps learn to like me a little, will you do that?'

'Well, I've almost always liked you,' said Venetia, 'and I've loved you for quite some time.'

She smiled then, and went into his arms to be kissed and kissed again, and Aunt Millicent, looking more like Miss Marple than ever before, nodded her neat head as she watched them from the window. Not that either of them would have minded—they were in their own happy world.

Take 4 bestselling love stories FREE

Plus get a FREE surprise gift!

Special Limited-time Offer

Harlequin Reader Service®

Mail to
In the U.S.
3010 Walden Avenue
P.O. Box 1867
Buffalo, N.Y. 14269-1867

In Canada
P.O. Box 609
Fort Erie, Ontario
L2A 5X3

YES! Please send me 4 free Harlequin Romance® novels and my free surprise gift. Then send me 6 brand-new novels every month, which I will receive months before they appear in bookstores. Bill me at the low price of $2.24* each—a savings of 26¢ apiece off cover prices. There are no shipping, handling or other hidden costs. I understand that accepting the books and gift places me under no obligation ever to buy any books. I can always return a shipment and cancel at any time. Even if I never buy another book from Harlequin, the 4 free books and the surprise gift are mine to keep forever.

*Offer slightly different in Canada—$2.24 per book plus 69¢ per shipment for delivery. Sales tax applicable in N.Y.

316 BPA WAV2 (CAN)

116 BPA FAWF (US)

Name _____ (PLEASE PRINT)

Address _____ Apt. No. _____

City _____ State/Prov. _____ Zip/Postal Code _____

This offer is limited to one order per household and not valid to present Harlequin Romance® subscribers. Terms and prices are subject to change.

© 1990 Harlequin Enterprises Limited

PASSPORT TO ROMANCE
SWEEPSTAKES RULES

1. **HOW TO ENTER:** To enter, you must be the age of majority and complete the official entry form, or print your name, address, telephone number and age on a plain piece of paper and mail to: Passport to Romance, P.O. Box 9056 Buffalo NY 14269-9056 No mechanically reproduced entries accepted.

2. All entries must be received by the CONTEST CLOSING DATE DECEMBER 31 1990 TO BE ELIGIBLE.

3. **THE PRIZES:** There will be ten (10) Grand Prizes awarded, each consisting of a choice of a trip for two people from the following list:
   - i) London, England (approximate retail value $5,050 U.S.)
   - ii) England, Wales and Scotland (approximate retail value $6,400 U.S.)
   - iii) Carribean Cruise (approximate retail value $7,300 U.S.)
   - iv) Hawaii (approximate retail value $9,550 U.S.)
   - v) Greek Island Cruise in the Mediterranean (approximate retail value $12,250 U.S.)
   - vi) France (approximate retail value $7,300 U.S.)

4. Any winner may choose to receive any trip or a cash alternative prize of $5,000.00 U.S. in lieu of the trip.

5. **GENERAL RULES:** Odds of winning depend on number of entries received.

6. A random draw will be made by Nielsen Promotion Services, an independent judging organization, on January 29, 1991, in Buffalo, NY. at 11:30 a.m. from all eligible entries received on or before the Contest Closing Date.

7. Any Canadian entrants who are selected must correctly answer a time-limited, mathematical skill-testing question in order to win.

8. Full contest rules may be obtained by sending a stamped, self-addressed envelope to: "Passport to Romance Rules Request", P.O. Box 9998, Saint John, New Brunswick, Canada E2L 4N4.

9. Quebec residents may submit any litigation respecting the conduct and awarding of a prize in this contest to the Régie des loteries et courses du Québec.

10. Payment of taxes other than air and hotel taxes is the sole responsibility of the winner.

11. Void where prohibited by law

COUPON BOOKLET OFFER TERMS

To receive your Free travel-savings coupon booklets, complete the mail-in Offer Certificate on the preceeding page, including the necessary number of proofs-of-purchase, and mail to: Passport to Romance, P.O. Box 9057, Buffalo, NY 14269-9057 The coupon booklets include savings on travel-related products such as car rentals, hotels, cruises, flowers and restaurants. Some restrictions apply. The offer is available in the United States and Canada. Requests must be postmarked by January 25, 1991. Only proofs-of-purchase from specially marked "Passport to Romance" Harlequin® or Silhouette® books will be accepted. The offer certificate must accompany your request and may not be reproduced in any manner. Offer void where prohibited or restricted by law. LIMIT FOUR COUPON BOOKLETS PER NAME, FAMILY, GROUP, ORGANIZATION OR ADDRESS. Please allow up to 8 weeks after receipt of order for shipment. Enter quickly as quantities are limited. Unfulfilled mail-in offer requests will receive free Harlequin® or Silhouette® books (not previously available in retail stores), in quantities equal to the number of proofs-of-purchase required for Levels One to Four, as applicable.

PR-SWPS

OFFICIAL SWEEPSTAKES
ENTRY FORM

Complete and return this Entry Form immediately—the more Entry Forms you submit, the better your chances of winning!
- Entry Forms must be received by **December 31, 1990**
- A random draw will take place on **January 29, 1991**
- Trip must be taken by **December 31, 1991**

3-HR-2-SW

YES, I want to win a PASSPORT TO ROMANCE vacation for two! I understand the prize includes round-trip air fare, accommodation and a daily spending allowance.

Name_____

Address_____

City_____ State_____ Zip_____

Telephone Number_____ Age_____

Return entries to: **PASSPORT TO ROMANCE**, P.O. Box 9056, Buffalo, NY 14269-9056

© 1990 Harlequin Enterprises Limited

COUPON BOOKLET/OFFER CERTIFICATE

Item	LEVEL ONE Booklet 1	LEVEL TWO Booklet 1 & 2	LEVEL THREE Booklet 1, 2 & 3	LEVEL FOUR Booklet 1, 2, 3 & 4
Booklet 1 = $100+	$100+	$100+	$100+	$100+
Booklet 2 = $200+		$200+	$200+	$200+
Booklet 3 = $300+			$300+	$300+
Booklet 4 = $400+	____	____	____	$400+
Approximate Total Value of Savings	$100+	$300+	$600+	$1,000+
# of Proofs of Purchase Required	4	6	12	18
Check One	____	____	____	____

Name_____

Address_____

City_____ State_____ Zip_____

Return Offer Certificates to: **PASSPORT TO ROMANCE**, P.O. Box 9057, Buffalo, NY 14269-9057

Requests must be postmarked by **January 25, 1991**

✂

ONE PROOF OF PURCHASE

3-HR-2

To collect your free coupon booklet you must include the necessary number of proofs-of-purchase with a properly completed Offer Certificate

© 1990 Harlequin Enterprises Limited

See previous page for details